"You're Going To Be My Hobby."

"I don't want to be your hobby," Elissa protested weakly. Her legs felt trembly.

"I was yours at the beginning," he reminded her. "You've no one to blame but yourself."

"That was different. You were repressed," she said defensively. He was too close. She was inhaling the tangy, clean scent of him, and it was intoxicating her more than the cocktail had. His bared chest was hard under her fingers, and between seeing him and smelling him and feeling him, she was adrift on sensation, her heart pounding. All that devastating masculinity, so close.

"*I* was repressed?" he asked with an amused smile.

Dear Reader,

Welcome to Silhouette! Our goal is to give you hours of unbeatable reading pleasure, and we hope you'll enjoy each month's six new Silhouette Desires. These sensual, provocative love stories are both believable and compelling—sometimes they're poignant, sometimes humorous, but always enjoyable.

Indulge yourself. Experience all the passion and excitement of falling in love along with our heroine as she meets the irresistible man of her dreams and together they overcome all obstacles in the path to a happy ending.

If this is your first Desire, I hope it'll be the first of many. If you're already a Silhouette Desire reader, thanks for your support! Look for some of your favorite authors in the coming months: Stephanie James, Diana Palmer, Dixie Browning, Ann Major and Doreen Owens Malek, to name just a few.

Happy reading!

Isabel Swift
Senior Editor

SDRL-7/85

DIANA PALMER
Fit for a King

Silhouette Desire

Published by Silhouette Books New York

America's Publisher of Contemporary Romance

For parrot people everywhere...

SILHOUETTE BOOKS
300 East 42nd St., New York, N.Y. 10017

Copyright © 1987 by Diana Palmer

ISBN: 0-373-05349-5

First Silhouette Books printing May 1987

America's Publisher of Contemporary Romance

Printed in the U.S.A.

DIANA PALMER

is a prolific romance writer who got her start as a newspaper reporter. Accustomed to the daily deadlines of a journalist, she has no problem with writer's block. In fact, she averages a book every two months. Mother of a young son, Diana met and married her husband within one week: "It was just like something from one of my books."

One

The king-size bed felt strange to Elissa, which was no surprise, really, since it wasn't her own. It belonged to Kingston Roper, and it was a good thing they were friends or
she'd never have done him this "little favor" on a minute's
notice. Elissa's own safe, single bed was in her little cottage
on the white Jamaican beach near Montego Bay, only a
short walk from King's enormous villa.

In the past two years Elissa knew she'd gone from being
just an irritating neighbor to the only friend King had. And
friend was the word; they certainly weren't lovers. Elissa
Gloriana Dean, for all her eccentricities and uninhibited
appearance, was an innocent. Her missionary parents had
given her a loving but restrictive upbringing, and not even
her budding success in the sophisticated world of fashion
design had liberated her in any physical way.

This trip down she'd been on the island only since that
morning, missing King, who wasn't at home, and half-

heartedly working on her newest collection of colorful lei-
sure wear for the boutique that carried her exclusive designs. Then, just an hour ago, King had phoned her with this
wild request and had hung up without a word of explana-
tion the moment she'd agreed to help him out. She couldn't
imagine why he wanted her to be found in his bed. He didn't
seem to be dating anyone. But then again, maybe he was
being hounded by some bored socialite and wanted to show
her that he was already involved. This tactic did seem a bit
drastic, though, especially since King was adept at speaking his mind. He never pulled his punches, even with people he liked. Oh, well. All the wondering in the world wasn't
going to give her any answers. She'd simply have to wait to
hear what King had to say.

She stretched luxuriously in his huge bed, the smooth
satin sheets feeling cool and sexy against her skin. She was
wearing a nightgown, but it was made of the finest cotton
and slit to the hips on both sides. In front, it made a plunge
to her navel. The daring pink negligee was part of her fantasy life, she admitted to herself. In some ways she might be
repressed on the surface, but in her mind she was a beautiful siren who lured men to their dooms.

Only with King could she safely indulge that fantasy
woman, however, because he never approached her physically. With King, she could flirt to heart's content. Although she was friendly to most men, she was careful not to
tease. The instant a man mistook her playful friendliness for
a come-on, she retreated into her shell, the fantasy shattered. It was one thing to pretend to be sexy, but quite another to follow through. A frightening experience in her
teens had left her extremely wary in that regard.

King was safe, though, Elissa reminded herself. Over the
past two years he'd become a friend and a confidant, and
she wasn't afraid to let down her guard with him. She
wouldn't have dreamed of wearing this revealing gown in
front of anyone else. But despite their sometimes flirtatious

camaraderie, King scarcely even seemed to notice that she *had* a body, so this little charade held no danger. She smiled to herself, feeling womanly and sexy and wildly come-hitherish. She would put on a great act for whoever this persistent female was, and later King could tell her all about it.

Kingston Roper, she mused. He could be such an enigma at times—like now. He was a big-time businessman, she knew—oil and gas and a few diversified interests, as she recalled. He'd inherited interest in the family company, which had been on the verge of bankruptcy, and had used his business savvy to make a fortune. Apparently his half brother, whose father had left the business to both sons, had been competing like mad to overtake King ever since.

Although they talked frequently and freely, she and King didn't spend a whole lot of time discussing everyday details about themselves, and as a result, she now realized, she didn't know all that much about his family. His half brother, Bobby, was married, and King had said something about expecting him and his wife for a visit. But that was at about the time she'd had to go back to the States to oversee her latest collection as it was assembled.

She smiled again as she thought about the success of that collection, which allowed her the luxury of spending time in Jamaica. Her name was her label—*Elissa*—and she catered to a unique clientele. Her sportswear was exotic, and its fantasy flair was designed to capture the eye as well as the imagination. She favored dramatic combinations of red and black and white, with the emphasis on cut and silhouette. Her styles had taken some time to catch on, but now that they had, sales were booming, and she was making a nice living. The cottage had been a godsend—she'd bought it at a terrific price when she'd been on a rare vacation—and for the past two years, whenever she needed rest or inspiration, she left the small Miami house she shared with her parents and came to sunny Jamaica.

She'd led a sheltered but happy life, one of the consequences of being the only child of former missionaries. Her
parents were highly individualistic and encouraged Elissa to
be the same—except in one respect. They were extremely
moral people, and they had instilled that same morality into
their daughter. As a result of her upbringing, Elissa was
something of a misfit in the modern world, but in most re-
spects—even in her wild designs—she was an individual.

When she came to Jamaica, she relaxed by watching out
for King, who seemed to be in almost permanent residence
these days. Two years ago she'd taken him on as a social
project, since he kept so much to himself, never smiled and
seemed to think about nothing except business. Gradually,
she reflected, he'd thawed a little. She grinned, then tensed,
listening carefully to the sounds coming from the next room.
Realizing it was only Warchief mumbling to himself in his
covered cage, she relaxed.

The big yellow-naped Amazon parrot belonged to Elissa,
but she'd never taken him to the States. He belonged on his
tropical island, and she loved him too much to risk disturbing his delicate immune system with the stress of interna-
tional travel. King seemed to like him well enough, since he
let the five-year-old parrot stay with him when Elissa was
away. Warchief had had a bad cold when she'd arrived in
Jamaica this time, and to avoid upsetting the bird with a
move while he was still sick, King was letting him stay at the
villa until he recovered. He'd be well soon, though; already
he was as feisty as ever.

It had been Warchief who'd first introduced them, she
remembered fondly. Elissa had nearly drained her bank account to buy the big green bird from his previous owner,
who'd been moving into an apartment. Warchief definitely
wasn't an apartment bird. He heralded dawn and dusk with
equal enthusiasm, and his ear-piercing cries did sound like
an Indian warrior of old on the attack. Hence, his name.

At the time, Elissa had been thoroughly ignorant of birds and hadn't known about this particular trait of Amazon parrots. She had taken Warchief to her cottage, and promptly at dusk she'd discovered why his former owner had been so enthusiastic about selling him.

Covering the cage had only made the parrot madder. She'd frantically thumbed through one of the old bird magazines she'd been given to an article on screaming, biting birds. Don't throw water on them, the article cautioned. If you do, instead of a screaming, biting bird, you'll have a *wet*, screaming, biting bird.

She'd sighed worriedly, gnawing on her lower lip as the parrot began to imitate a police siren. Or could it be the real thing? Perhaps her new neighbor in that big white villa had called the Jamaican police?

At that point a loud, angry knock on the front door had startled her. "Hush, Warchief!" she'd pleaded.

He'd squawked even louder, rattling the bars of his cage like a convict bent on escape.

"Oh, for heaven's sake!" she'd wailed, holding her ears and peeking out the curtain before she opened the door.

But it hadn't been the police. It was worse. It was the cold, hard, mean-looking man who lived in that huge white villa down the beach. The man who looked as intimidating as a stone wall and walked like a bulldozer hunting hills. He seemed furious, and Elissa wondered if she could get away with pretending she wasn't home.

"Open this door, or the police will," a deep, Western-accented voice boomed.

With a resigned sigh, she unlocked it. He was tall, whip-cord lean and dangerous looking, from his tousled dark hair and his half-opened tropical shirt to the white shorts that emphasized the deep tan and pure muscle of his long legs. He had a chest that would have started fires in a more liberated woman than Elissa. It was very broad, with a thick wedge of black hair that curled down past the waistband around his lean hips. His face was chiseled looking, rough and masculine, with a straight nose and a cruelly sensuous mouth. There wasn't an ounce of fat on him, and he smelled of tangy cologne—expensive, probably, if that Rolex buried in the thick hair on his wrist and the big diamond ring on his darkly tanned hand were any indication of material worth. He made her feel like a midget, even though she was considered tall herself.

"Yes?" She smiled, trying to bluff her way through his obvious animosity.

"What the hell's going on over here?" he asked curtly.

She blinked. "I beg your pardon?"

"I heard screams," he said, his very dark, almost black, eyes staring intently at her face.

"Well, yes, they were screams, but—" she began.

"I bought my house specifically for its peaceful location," he broke in before she could finish. "I like peace and quiet. I came all the way here from Oklahoma to get it. I don't like wild parties."

"Oh, neither do I," she said earnestly.

At which point Warchief let out a scream that could have shattered crystal.

"Why is that woman screaming? What in hell kind of company are you keeping here, lady?" The man from Oklahoma spared her a speaking glance before he pushed past her into the cottage and began looking for the source of the scream.

She sighed, leaning against the doorjamb as he strode into the bedroom, then the small kitchen, muttering about bloody murder and the lack of consideration for the neighbors on this side of the island.

Warchief began laughing in an absurd parody of a man's deep voice, and then he screamed again, his tone rising alarmingly.

The Oklahoman was back, hands on his narrow hips, scowling. And then his eyes found the covered cage.

"Helllllllp!" Warchief moaned, and the man's eyebrows shot up his forehead.

"The wild party," she informed him calmly, "is in there. And *wild* is really a good word for that particular party."

"Ouuuuut!" the parrot wailed. "Let me out!"

The Oklahoman pulled off the dark cover, and Warchief immediately began making eyes at him. "Hello!" he purred, leaping from his perch ring to the cage door. "I'm a good boy. Who are you?"

The tall man blinked. "It's a parrot."

"I'm a good boy," Warchief said, and he laughed again. As an encore he turned upside down, cocking his head at the man. "You're cute!"

Cute wasn't exactly the word Elissa would have used, but that parrot had style—she'd say that for him. She covered her mouth with her hand to keep from laughing.

Warchief spread his tail feathers and ruffled the rest of himself, dilated his pale brown eyes in what bird fanciers call "blazing" and let out a beaut of a wail. The stranger from Oklahoma raised one heavy eyebrow. "How would you like him," he asked darkly, glancing at her, "fried or baked stuffed?"

"You can't!" she moaned. "He's just a baby!"

The parrot let out another bloodcurdling scream.

"Down, boy!" the man growled. "I don't have my ears insured."

Elissa muffled a giggle. "He's terrific, isn't he?" she asked gleefully. "Now I see why his owner had to sell him when he moved into a small apartment building. I didn't realize it until the sun started going down."

The intruder stared at the pile of bird magazines on the glass-topped coffee table. "Well? Haven't you learned yet what to do about his screaming?"

"Of course," she replied, tongue in cheek. "You cover the cage. It works every time. This expert—" she held up the magazine "—says so."

He glanced at the cover of the magazine. "That issue is three years old."

She shrugged. "Can I help it if bird magazines aren't exactly the going thing on the island? The owner gave these to me along with the cage."

His eyes told her what he thought of the magazines, the cage and the bird in it. Her, too.

"So he screams a little," she defended, shifting under that hot glare. "Basically he's a nice bird. He'll even let you pet him."

He eyed the bird. "Want to show me?"

"Not really." But at the man's baleful glance, she moved closer and held out her hand. The parrot cackled and made a playful swipe at it. She jerked her hand back. "Well, he'll almost let you pet him," she equivocated.

"Care to try again?" he challenged, folding his darkly tanned arms across that massive chest.

She put her hands behind her. "No, thanks. I've kind of gotten used to having ten fingers," she muttered.

"No doubt. What in heaven's name do you want with a parrot, anyway?" he asked, clearly exasperated.

"I was lonely," she said bluntly. She glanced down at her bare feet.

"Why not take a lover?" he returned.

She looked up and saw that his eyes were full of what looked like mischief. "Take him where?" she asked glibly, hiding the uncomfortable reaction his suggestion evoked from her.

A corner of his firm mouth seemed to twitch. "Cute."

"You're cute!" Warchief echoed, and he began to strut in a circle, fluffed up like a cat in a dryer, screaming his lime-green head off. Even the streak of yellow on his nape seemed to glow.

"For Pete's sake, boy!" the man burst out.

"Maybe he's a girl," Elissa commented. "He sure seems to like you a lot."

He glared at Warchief. "I don't like the way he's looking at me," he commented. "I feel like an entrée."

"His former owner promised he wouldn't bite," she faltered.

"Sure he did." He held out his hand, and Warchief seemed to actually grin before he reached through the wide cage bars for it.

He wasn't a malicious bird; he just liked to test his strength, Elissa rationalized. But the man from Oklahoma had strong fingers. He let Warchief bear down for a minute before he leisurely removed the big beak and firmly said, "No!"

He picked up the cage cover and put it back in place. And to Elissa's amazement, the parrot shut up.

"You have to let an animal know who's boss," he told Elissa. "Never jerk your hand back if he starts to bite, and don't let him get away with it. You'll only reinforce his bad behavior."

She blinked. "You seem to know a lot about birds."

"I had a cockatoo," he told her. "I gave it to a friend of mine because I'm away so much of the time."

"You're from Oklahoma, you said?" she asked, curious.

He cocked an eyebrow. "Yes."

"I'm from Florida," she said with a smile. "I design sportswear for a chain of boutiques." She peeked up at him. "I could design you a great sun dress."

He glowered at her. "First the parrot, now this. I don't know which is worse, lady, you or the last woman who lived here."

"The woman I bought the cottage from?" she recalled, frowning. "What was wrong with her?"

"She liked to sunbathe nude when I was swimming," he muttered darkly.

She grinned, remembering the woman very well. She was about fifty years old, at least a size twenty and only five feet tall.

"It's not funny," he commented.

"Yes, it is," she laughed.

But he still didn't smile. Despite his earlier flip remarks, he looked like a man who hadn't much use for humor.

"I've got three hours of work left before I can sleep," he said curtly, turning away. "From now on, cover that bird when he starts whooping. He'll get the message sooner or later. And don't keep him up late. It isn't good for him. Birds need twelve hours each of daylight and dark."

"Yes, sir. Thank you, sir. Anything else, sir?" she asked pertly as she skipped along beside him to the door.

He stopped short, his dark eyes threatening. "How old are you, anyway? Past the age of consent?"

"I'm a candidate for the old folks' home, in fact." She grinned. "I'm pushing twenty-six. Still about twenty years your junior, though, I'll bet, old man."

He looked stunned, as if no one had ever dared speak to him in such a manner. "I'm thirty-nine," he said absently.

"You look more like forty-five," she sighed, studying his hard, care-creased face. "I'll bet you take five-hour vacations and count your money every night. You have that look, you know." His eyebrows shot up, and she wiggled hers. "Rich and miserable?"

"I'm filthy rich, but I'm not miserable."

"Yes, you are," she told him. "You just don't realize it. But don't worry. Now that I'm around, I'll save you from yourself. In no time you'll be a new man."

"I like me fine the way I am," he said tersely, glaring down at her. "So don't pester me. I don't care to be remodeled, least of all by some bored textile worker."

"I'm a designer," she shot back.

"You can't possibly be old enough." He patted her on the head, the first glimpse of real humor she'd seen in him. "Go to bed, child."

"Mind you don't trip over your long beard, Grandpa," she called after him.

He didn't look back or say another word. He just kept walking.

And that had been the beginning of an odd friendship. In the months that followed, Elissa had learned precious few actual facts about her taciturn neighbor, but she'd gleaned a great deal about his temperament. His full name was Kingston, and no one called him King. Except Elissa. He spent most of his waking hours on business. Although he traveled extensively, his home base was Jamaica because few people except those who really needed to, knew how to get in touch with him there. He liked his privacy and avoided the social gatherings that seemed de rigueur for the Americans in their exclusive part of Montego Bay. He kept to himself and spent his rare free time walking on the beach, alone and apparently liking it. He might have gone on for years that way. But Elissa had saved him from himself.

Although she didn't trust most men, she instinctively trusted King. He seemed totally uninterested in her as a woman, and when weeks went by without his making a suggestive remark or a pass, she began to feel totally safe with him. That allowed her to indulge her fantasy of being the sophisticated, worldly kind of woman she liked to read about in novels. It was an illusion, of course, but King didn't seem to mind her outrageous flirting and sometimes suggestive remarks. He treated her much like a young girl, alternately indulging and teasing her. And that was fine with Elissa. She'd long since learned that she wouldn't fit easily into the modern world. She couldn't bring herself to sleep with a man just because it was the fashion. And since most men she dated expected that courtesy, she simply withdrew. She never took a date home—not anymore, at least. There had been a nice man when she was twenty. A real jewel, she'd thought—until she took him home to meet Mom and Dad. She'd never seen him again.

For all her religious outlook on life, her parents were characters. Her father collected lizards, and her mother was a special deputy with the sheriff's department. Odd people. Lovely but very odd. Since she'd given up on expecting tolerance from the opposite sex, she couldn't imagine a male friend really understanding her delightful family. So it was a good thing she'd decided to die a virgin.

Fortunately, King had no designs on her whatsoever, so he was good company and a hedge against other men when she was on the island. He was the perfect safe harbor. Not only that, but he needed a little attention to keep him from becoming a hermit. And who better to draw him out than Elissa, given her somewhat evangelical background?

At first she contented herself with leaving little notes for him to find, exhorting pithy things like "Too much loneliness makes a man odd" or "Sunstroke can be hazardous to your health." She put the notes on his front door, on the windshield of his car, even under the rock where he liked to sit and watch the sunset. From there, she took bolder steps. She baked things for him. She put flowers on his doorstep.

Eventually, he came over to tell her to stop—and found her waiting for him with an elaborate meal. Clearly it was the last straw, and he gave up trying to ignore her. After that, he came to eat at least once a week, and sometimes they walked on the beach together. Despite her outgoing approach, she was a little wary of him at first, until he proved by his attitude that he wasn't going to try to get her into the nearest available bed. And then he became her friend. She totally relaxed with him and looked forward to their times together. He seemed pleased enough with that arrangement himself, talking to her as if she were a sister.

When she went back to the States to work, he generously offered to keep Warchief. She'd been delighted, and King had given the bird a nice substitute home. When he was out of the country on business, he even hired a woman to look after the house and the bird. For all his hardness, he had a soft center—if one looked closely enough. He was still impatient and demanding with most people—Elissa had once had her ears curled listening to him chew out a subordinate—but he seemed to tolerate her better than he tolerated others.

The only puzzling thing about him was his lack of a love life. He was devastatingly handsome and physically near perfect. At his age, she'd have expected him to be married. But he wasn't and evidently never had been. He dated occasionally, but Elissa never spotted him bringing a woman home overnight. Even in her innocence Elissa knew it was rather unusual for a man who was so much a man to spend so much time alone. She wondered about it frequently, and once she even got up enough courage to quiz him on the subject. But his face had closed up, and he'd changed the subject. She hadn't asked again.

Despite her innate curiosity, she was relieved that he'd never once made a pass at her. She had some hang-ups from an experience that her parents didn't even know about, thank God. One wild party, attended without their knowledge, had cured her of any wanton imaginings. She'd barely escaped with her innocence intact, and she'd gleaned a very unpleasant, threatening picture of the aroused male. She'd been careful ever since.

She was only grateful that her parents weren't in any danger of dropping in at the Roper villa. If they'd seen her in King's bed ... Then she laughed, remembering how they were. They knew her so well that they'd have asked what was the joke. How marvelous having parents like hers, idiosyncrasies and all.

King was due any minute, and Elissa's part in this practical joke was simply to lie back and look loved. She wasn't sure why he wanted to give that impression, or to whom, but he'd once saved her from the unwanted attention of a very persistent insurance salesman, so now she was saving him. From something. Really, though, he was going to owe her a steak dinner for all this bother.

She heard the front door open, and voices drifted down the hall. She recognized King's, and for one wild second she let herself pretend that she was waiting for him as a lover. The thought didn't terrify her, and that puzzled her. In fact, her body began to tingle in the oddest ways, and that *really* puzzled her.

Then the bedroom door opened, and King stared at her over the head of the most beautiful blonde Elissa had ever seen.

The blonde wore a look of helpless longing and unholy torment. And King's expression was a revelation as he glanced down at her. For a face that rarely gave away a trace of emotion, it was suddenly explicit with tender interest. Who was the woman? Elissa wondered. And why would King want to discourage her when he was so obviously attracted to her?

Elissa was so confused that she almost forgot to play her part. This vulnerability in King was so expected. But there must be a reason he wanted that lovely woman with him to think he was involved with someone else, and this was obviously no time to ask questions.

"Well, hello, darling," Elissa said in her best husky voice. She tugged the covers up demurely and yawned delicately. "I fell asleep again," she added meaningfully, and she waited for the blonde to react.

Two

The reaction was almost instantaneous. "Oh!" The woman faltered, stopping beside King as if frozen to the spot. She stared at Elissa with huge, soft eyes, clearly struggling to find words, and her delicate skin colored, making her even more beautiful. "Ex-excuse me."

"I didn't expect you to still be here, Elissa," King said with a smile that was obviously forced.

Elissa played her part to perfection, letting her eyes droop sleepily. "I'm sorry if I've overstayed my welcome."

"Don't be absurd," he replied. "There's no reason you shouldn't stay if you like. Bess, do you mind...?" he asked the blonde. "There's a guest bathroom just down the hall."

"I'll...I'll use that one, of course." She looked totally flustered, Elissa noted sympathetically. "Excuse me," she whispered, her voice almost breaking. She turned and nearly ran down the hall.

King closed the door and leaned back against it, his face without expression, his dark eyes looking at Elissa without really seeming to see her. He never gave away much, but that hard face was faintly pale under its rugged tan.

Elissa climbed out of bed, oblivious to her state of undress. He wasn't looking, anyway. He paid very little attention to her as a rule, and if she'd wondered why in the past, she now had a suspicion. She went to stand in front of him, her head back, her eyes curious.

"Okay," she said. "Why don't you tell me all about it? I'm a clam when I need to be, and you look as if you need a friend pretty badly."

His jaw tightened. He looked down into her blue eyes, and she could see his control waver, just for an instant, before he got it back. "That's Bess," he said finally. "My brother's wife," he added significantly. After a pause, he continued tonelessly, "He'll be along in an hour or so; he's still in a business meeting."

She remembered his mentioning Bobby and Bess, and she also remembered that he never talked much about them. Now she had a sneaking hunch she knew why. Her eyes narrowed as she took in his look of utter dejection.

"Is one of you in hot pursuit of the other?" she conjectured, smiling gently at his faint surprise. "Since I'm guessing, *she's* after *you*, I imagine, and that's why I was shanghaied into decorating your bed."

"It isn't quite that simple," he murmured, searching her wide eyes.

"Why don't you try telling me about it?" she suggested softly.

Still gazing intently at her, he seemed to consider that possibility, took a deep breath and then began. "They came down month before last while Bobby was working to get a hotel complex started. He's been deeply involved in negotiations, and now he's finalizing the subcontracting bids," he explained. He paused.

"Go on," Elissa prompted gently.

"Bess has been lonely, so instead of going back to Oklahoma, she's been depending on me for amusement." He stopped, then continued haltingly, "But a couple of nights ago, the amusement did a disappearing act, and things started to get serious." Again he stopped, then rushed on. "So I started grasping at straws and told her I was involved with you. If you hadn't sent me that letter asking me to get the utilities on, I might still be in hot water. But I knew you'd be in tonight, so I made sure Bess would come over. To catch you in a compromising situation, that is."

"Too bad I wasn't stark naked instead, then," she said lightly, trying to cheer him up. She gave him a wicked smile. "Just picture it: gorgeous me in my birthday suit sprawled out on your satin sheets. That would have really caught her eye."

Oddly enough, that picture made King go hot all over. He suddenly realized he'd never really thought of Elissa as a woman before. She was so young, so naive, so trusting. She was like a little sister to him. But now, as his dark eyes wandered over her, he realized with a start that she was pretty sexy in that gown, and he wasn't thinking brotherly thoughts at all. He blinked. Maybe he was getting old and his glands were going crazy. Either that or his confusion over Bess was getting to him. In an effort to ground himself in reality once more, he reached out and clasped her shoulders. It was a mistake—they were bare.

Elissa started. It was a rare thing for King to touch her, and she was amazed at the pleasure the feel of his hands on her bare skin gave her.

"I think this will do it," he mused, even more confused yet relieved he could still find voice to respond to her joking remark. "Temporarily, at least. How about joining us for drinks, just for an hour or so? Just until Bobby gets here?"

He sounded almost desperate, and Elissa grinned. "Sure. What are friends for?" she said easily. She wondered how much he really cared for Bess and if his only motive in the charade was to ward off his sister-in-law. Perhaps he needed a barrier against his own impulses, too, to keep himself honest? Hard to tell; he could be such a poker face. At times she wondered if she really knew him at all. She searched his dark eyes, frowning slightly. ''King, is she in love with you?''

''I don't think she knows, Elissa,'' he said, his voice quiet and tense. ''She's lonely and bored—maybe a bit afraid, as well. Bobby leaves her alone too much. I'm not sure if she's really interested in me or just using me as a ploy to get Bobby's attention.''

In fact, he was afraid to take a chance on Bess's developing any real feeling for him, since he was having a hard enough time resisting her now. But he wasn't admitting any of that to Elissa.

He'd always had a soft spot for his sister-in-law, he acknowledged. Few people in her current social circle knew how rough she'd had it, what with a father who drank and kept her mother pregnant all the time. Bess hadn't even owned a decent dress when Bobby brought her home and announced that they were getting married. King had formed an immediate affection for the shy little blonde, and that tenderness had held on for the past ten years. Now it was hard to decide whether it was still brotherly affection or something more. Bess had never actively encouraged him before now.

Elissa caught the wistful look in King's eyes. Her lips pursed. ''Did you ever have something going with her, maybe before Bobby did?'' she probed gently.

He shook his head. ''She was just eighteen when they married. They were the same age, in fact.'' He shrugged. ''I was already eleven years her senior. Besides, Bobby saw her first.'' He laughed, then instantly sobered. ''They were close in those early days, when Bobby was working his way up in the business world. But now, with their years of living high on the hog and with the oil industry depressed, money's gotten a little tight." He frowned, studying her. "You know, I think maybe Bobby's working himself like crazy because he's afraid Bess won't want him if he can't support her in the style she's gotten accustomed to. And because he's ignoring her in his pursuit of new building contracts, she thinks he doesn't care."

"What a mess," she sighed.

"You aren't kidding. And guess who's smack-dab in the middle of it?" he asked ruefully. "They've gotten along pretty well the past ten years, but then, there was always lots of money. Bess used to joke about leaving him if he ever lost his shirt; she said she never wanted to be poor again. I don't think she really meant it about leaving him, but Bobby tends to take things literally, and they don't seem to talk much anymore. Anyway, I helped Bobby make some real-estate contacts here in Jamaica, and two months ago they came down to get things started. Bobby's been hellishly busy, so for the past few weeks Bess has turned to me—out of boredom, I'm sure. At first I suspected she wanted to use me to get Bobby to notice her again—you know, make him a little jealous. But it's getting complicated now." He shrugged, smiling faintly. "She's always been special to me, and I'm only human, if you get my meaning. But I don't want anyone to get hurt. That's where you come in."

"I'm going to run interference, I gather?" she murmured.

"That's it," he agreed pleasantly. "By the way, you've been in the States for the past few months because we had a quarrel. But now we've patched it up, and we're quite serious about each other."

"I'm beginning to see the light," she mused, grinning. "So we're lovers, is that it?"

He chuckled. "Can't keep our hands off each other," he agreed. "Mad to be together."

"What fun." She smiled. "Now explain my missionary parents to her and how you so easily led me into a life of sin."

He groaned. "Don't, for heaven's sake, even mention your parents to her. Well, not what they do for a living, at least."

She sighed. "I hope she doesn't pin me down and start asking embarrassing questions."

"I'll try not to leave you alone with her. You've got to save me," he murmured dryly, although there seemed to be something serious behind the gibe. "Bobby and I are getting along better than we ever have. I can't come between him and the one thing in life he really values."

She sighed. "Okay. I'll play along. But I have to go back to the States in about three weeks, so you'd better get her convinced fast."

"They'll be going back any day now, I hope," he said. "Otherwise I don't know if I can stand it much longer. It's a good thing I saw your lights on before Bobby got me to pick up Bess at their villa. I barely had time to pressure you into cooperating before I had to leave."

"Lucky you," she agreed with a grin. "I hadn't planned to come back for two more weeks."

He groaned. "I'd have been in over my head by then, for sure."

She glanced up at him. "Well, don't you worry. I'll save you." She frowned, moving away from the disturbing touch of his hands. "Let's see now, what did I do with that red cape—you know, the one with the big *S* on it?"

"Never mind the Superwoman cape," he said. "Just hold my hand."

"The one with the Rolex and the diamond ring?" She pursed her lips. "Careful I don't steal them. I'm not rich yet, you know."

He laughed. "You will be," he said. Then he glanced toward the door. "Get dressed, will you? I'll wait for you."

Heavens, he had it bad, Elissa thought, if he was afraid to face the other woman without reinforcements.

"Chin up," she said lightly. "I know karate. If she makes one move—just one move—to undress you, I'll defend your honor with my very life.'

He chuckled. Once, he'd thought his new neighbor was a complete eccentric. He still did, actually, but she could be quite a gem at times, too. And right now she was saving his neck. "You're a nice girl," he said playfully.

She winced. "A nice girl? Thanks awfully. I like you, too."

She turned, picked up her clothes from the chair and headed toward the bathroom.

"You can't dress in front of me?" he asked unexpectedly, watching her from his relaxed position against the door.

She glanced up at him. "No," she confessed with a somewhat wobbly laugh. "I'm not quite as liberated as I might seem. I—I've never undressed in front of a man in my life, except for my family physician."

The confession seemed to shock him. "Never?" he asked.

"Never," she emphasized, knowing exactly what she was revealing to him.

He scowled. Because of her physical aloofness, he'd somehow taken it for granted that she'd been hurt in love somehow. To think of her as a virgin was vaguely disturbing.

"Why?" he asked with charasteristic bluntness. "Did something happen to you?"

"My father's a minister, remember? And he and my mother were missionaries to Brazil when I was growing up. Try being Ms. Liberation in that kind of atmosphere. I dare you."

He was learning more about her in minutes than he'd learned in two years. He studied her intently, his gaze taking in what he could see of her body in that very revealing gown. Her breasts were full and firm looking, her minuscule waist flared into nicely rounded hips, and she had long, nicely shaped legs. Her face was lovely. And that teasing, provocative air of hers, he realized, was pretty false at times. Remembering that he'd seen her actually back away when men came too close physically, he regarded her thoughtfully.

"No wonder," he mumbled.

"No wonder what?" she echoed.

"Well, I'd always thought of you as sophisticated," he mused, thinking of her occasional flirtatiousness. "You certainly don't act like a virgin. And yet—"

"How does a virgin act, for heaven's sake?" she broke in. "Stand on the edge of a volcano and jump in?"

Despite the seriousness of his current predicament, King found himself laughing, and it dawned on him that he laughed more with Elissa than he ever had in his life. But then, his path hadn't been an easy one. Part Indian, he'd grown up fighting two worlds. Most people didn't even know that he and Bobby had different fathers. Bobby's was a Texas oilman who'd left his business equally to both boys. King's father was a full-blooded Apache whose ill-fated attempt to fit into his wife's social set had been a disaster. A marriage of rich and poor might make good novels, but it was hard work in real life. Eventually, King's father had walked out the door in the middle of one too many cocktail parties and vanished. King had never seen him again. His mother had remarried, and when Bobby came along, there seemed to be little affection left for the elder son. He learned to fight his own battles, because he got no coddling. He'd spent his whole life fighting. He guessed that in many ways he was still fighting.

"You almost never laugh," Elissa pointed out, holding her jump suit against her breasts.

"Oh, now and again I do. With you." He smiled. "Go get dressed, walking sacrifice. I'll wait out here."

She studied him quietly, curious about the worn expression on his face. More than Bess was troubling him, she sensed. She wondered briefly if being the product of two worlds ever bothered him. She knew about his Indian ancestry; in her typical outspoken fashion she'd once asked him why he was so dark. He'd given her the answer abruptly and changed the subject, clearly unwilling to discuss it. She sighed. What an enigma. She smiled back at him and went into the bathroom to change.

She put on one of her own creations, a slinky black jump suit with a red bodice and single strappy sleeve, and ran a brush through her long hair. She probably wouldn't wear the outfit around anybody except King. Another part of her fantasy life, she thought, and grinned at her reflection. She realized then that her lipstick was in her purse, so she went back into the bedroom to get it.

"Oh, fudge," she muttered, fumbling through the contents. "I don't even have a lipstick." She lifted her eyebrows in a speaking look, expecting him to read her mind, as usual. And he did.

"Sorry, I never use the stuff myself," he said dryly. "Do you really need one?" he asked, shouldering himself away from the door, a cigarette in his hand. He didn't often smoke, but tonight was unsettling him.

"Your sexy sister-in-law will be sure to notice if I don't make myself as beautiful as possible," she teased.

He came close to her, towering over her and letting his eyes wander with uncharacteristic boldness down her slender body. "If you'd put lipstick on," he murmured, "probably I'd have kissed it off by now, don't you think?"

Her heart jumped up into her throat at the unfamiliar look in those dark eyes. They searched her face, only to drop and linger on her full breasts, and suddenly she wished her neckline were a bit higher. He hadn't seemed to notice her body in the very revealing nightgown, but he was unusually attentive now.

"We shouldn't keep your sister-in-law waiting," she said. For the first time, he was making her nervous. Eyeing him warily, she walked around him, her composure starting to shatter. As usual, when a man came on too strong, she began to draw into her shell.

His lean hand shot out unexpectedly, and he drew her toward him, clamping her waist so that she couldn't move away.

That proximity was new and a little frightening, and she looked up into his dark eyes uncomprehendingly. "What are you doing?" she asked nervously.

"Trying to ruffle you a little," he murmured darkly. "You're too neat and pretty to go out there and convince Bess we're lovers."

"All right, then, how's this?" She ran her hand roughly through her hair.

He shook his head. "Not good enough." His eyes dropped to her soft mouth, and for the first time in their relationship he wondered how it would feel to have that soft mouth under his lips.

She felt his strong fingers bite into her waist, and her eyes widened. "Hold it, now, big fella," she cautioned gently. "I'm not on the menu, remember?"

His eyebrows rose curiously. "Are you afraid of me, tidbit?" he asked in a tone he'd never used before. It was deep and slow and sultry, like the look in his dark, faintly amused eyes.

"That doesn't enter into it," she replied. "I won't let you use me for real. I won't substitute for your sister-in-law, King."

His face hardened. "I don't recall asking you to," he returned curtly, releasing her.

"Good. As long as it's just an act, we'll get along fine," she said sweetly, although her legs were wobbling from his unexpected nearness. She could almost drown in that heady, expensive cologne of his, which clung to her skin from just that brief contact with him. The situation was far too intimate, and she quickly changed the subject to divert them both. "Is Bobby anything like you?" she asked. "I've never met him, you know. They were always back in Oklahoma when I was down here."

"We don't look a lot alike," he mused after a minute, finishing his cigarette. "You'll see for yourself soon enough."

She forced a smile. "Don't worry so much," she said, attempting to ease his obvious anxiety. "They'll leave soon, and you'll get your life back together."

With a rough sigh, he put out the cigarette and stuck his hands into his pockets. "I hate being in this position," he said unexpectedly, glaring toward the door.

"Doesn't your brother pay her any attention at all?" she asked quietly.

"He's very competitive," he replied. "He doesn't like running a close second to me. He never has. With the oil glut bringing the price of crude down, we've both had to diversify. But I've done it with more success than he has. Now he's going to catch up or kill himself. Unfortunately, Bess has become a casualty."

"Do they have children?"

He grimaced. "Bobby wanted to wait until they were completely secure."

"Aren't they, by now?" she probed gently.

He glanced at her. "They're comfortable, but they've gotten used to credit in a big way. Bess has diamonds and a sports car, but it could all go up in smoke tomorrow. That's how close they're living. Bobby's scared, and with good reason. This Jamaica project will either pull him out or break him, and he knows that, too."

Elissa didn't say anything, but she felt sorry for Bess. For a wife, the worst thing in the world must be having a husband who never noticed her. Elissa's parents were always together at home, even if they were doing different things.

They might be apart physically, but when they looked at each other, you knew that they were always one.

"Talking about it won't solve this problem," he said after a minute. "You don't mind carrying out the charade?" he added, raising his eyes.

"Not at all," she said, smiling gamely. "I've always wanted to try my hand at acting." She struck a pose, the back of her hand across her eyes. "I vant to be alone!"

"You imp," he chuckled. He shook his head on a sigh. "You're a puzzle, little miss designer," he murmured, watching her narrowly. "I'm amazed that no enterprising young man has ever seduced you."

She shrugged. "Most young men don't like seducing a minister's daughter," she said pertly. Her eyes twinkled. "I almost got in trouble one time, defying my folks. It hurt my conscience and frightened me a little, but I bounced back."

"Did you really?" he mused. "Then why are you still a virgin?"

"Because you don't undo twenty-five years of conditioning overnight," she replied easily. She searched his dark eyes. "If I ever did let a man seduce me, though, I'd want him to be like you."

His heart stopped. He couldn't think of a single thing to say as the thought worked on him and made his body react in a shocking way.

She shifted, embarrassed at her own boldness, although his stony face didn't give away a thing. "Sorry. I didn't mean to embarrass you. I just meant that you're a special kind of man. I know you'd never have to hurt a woman to feed your ego." She sighed. "I guess you've probably forgotten more about sex than I've ever learned."

"I guess I have, honey," he said, studying her down-bent head with a slight frown. He caught her hand in his—offering a small measure of comfort, he told himself. "We'd better go out."

At his strong, possessively warm touch, which set her palm to tingling, she looked up and met his searching gaze. It was like electricity. Startling. Unnerving. Her very breathing seemed to be affected by it.

"Yes," she said absently. His mouth was beautiful in a very masculine way, and she couldn't seem to stop looking at it.

He touched her long hair gently, his eyes still probing hers. She was trembling, he noticed in amazement. Then he looked down at the bodice of her jump suit and was surprised to find her nipples hard against the fabric—very obviously there was no bra beneath it. Suddenly he wanted to smooth his hands over her breasts. He wanted to taste her warm mouth and feel her body yield against the strength of his. His eyes narrowed at his own disturbing thoughts.

"I wish you wouldn't look at me that way," she said with that irrepressible honesty that had always intrigued him. "It . . . it makes me feel shaky."

His eyes rose to hers once more. "When I look at your breasts, you mean?" he asked gently.

Her lips opened on a shocked breath. He'd never spoken to her that way.

He could have bitten his tongue. What in hell was wrong with him? This was Elissa; they'd been friends for a long time. It was Bess who was getting to him. He sighed, wondering why he'd never before really noticed this little imp with her exquisite body and lovely face.

"I didn't mean to say that," he said vaguely. He dropped her hand, turned away from her abruptly and lit another cigarette. "I'm in a hell of a situation. I guess I'm more disturbed than I realized. Come on. Let's get it over with."

"All right." She followed him, her mind whirling. Had he been drinking? Would that explain his odd behavior? Perhaps wanting Bess had worked on his mind long enough to disorient him. That had to be it. He'd looked at her and he'd seen Bess. It was nothing to worry about.

"You're sure about this?" he asked before he opened the door.

"Of course," she assured him.

He sighed. "Well, let's see if we can carry it off." He held out his hand again.

She slid her slender fingers into it, a hesitant, but trusting, "Okay." She looked up, batting her lashes. "Oh, Kingston, you're so sexxxxxxy!" she drawled.

He laughed unexpectedly. "Cut it out. You're supposed to convince her."

"I guess I can try," she sighed. "You lead; I'll follow."

Bess was sitting on the edge of a chair, glancing toward the hallway when they emerged. The blonde's very blue eyes narrowed and there was real hostility in them for an instant before she skillfully erased it.

"I didn't know King had a...a girlfriend," Bess said, deliberately hesitating over the word. She smiled with sleek sophistication. "He said you'd had a quarrel and went back to Florida. But you seem to have made up."

"Oh, in the most delicious ways, too, haven't we, darling?" she asked King with a fluttering of her long lashes.

He chuckled. "I guess so," he mused, but he didn't look at Bess.

"Where in Florida do you live?" Bess continued.

"In Miami, most of the year," Elissa replied. She let go of King's hand and smiled at the older woman. "I understand you're married to King's brother?"

Bess glanced down at the drink she'd poured herself. "Yes. I'm Bobby's wife."

"You're cuuuuute!" Warchief burst out, circling his cage with appropriate whistles and clicks.

Bess stared at the big parrot. "You flirt," she accused the bird, forcing a smile.

Elissa relaxed a little. Bess wasn't so bad; at least she liked parrots. "He likes women," she explained, "but he's really in love with King. When I take him home, he mourns."

"Oh. He's yours?" Bess asked.

"Yes. He stays with King when I'm in the States, and I've only been back since this morning."

King glanced at her quickly. "Want a drink?"

"Yes, thank you," Elissa said. She read him very well. He was warning her not to let too much slip. She smiled. "Do you have pets, Bess?"

The other woman shook her head. "No pets. No kids." She sounded oddly wistful. She laughed, a hollow, haunting melody. "No nothing. It's just me and Bobby—when Bobby's ever home."

"Hard times, Bess," King reminded her. "If he doesn't keep on the ball, you'll have to give up your diamonds."

"It wasn't the diamonds I married him for, but he won't believe that," Bess replied. She looked up, her eyes searching King's face with what looked like pure longing. "Remember how it used to be, in the old days? Bobby and I would go to amusement parks and spend hours on the rides. Sometimes you'd take an afternoon off and come with us, and we'd stuff ourselves with ice cream and cotton candy...."

"It isn't wise to look back." He handed a vodka and tonic to Elissa.

"It isn't wise to look ahead, either," Bess replied miserably. "All I do is sit in hotel rooms these days...or sit at home alone." She glared at her drink. "It's a miracle I'm not an alcoholic."

"Don't you have a job or anything to keep you busy?" Elissa asked without thinking. At Bess's obvious chagrin, she hastily added, "I'm sorry, that sounded like a criticism, but honestly it wasn't. I just meant, if you had a project or a hobby, it might be less of a strain to be alone at times."

"I don't know how to do anything," Bess said sadly. "I married fresh out of high school, so I never really learned how to do much...besides be a wife."

The irony of Bess's situation wasn't lost on Elissa. "We can all do something," she said gently. "Paint or write or play an instrument or do crafts...."

"I used to play the piano," Bess replied. She looked down at her hands. "I was pretty good, too. But Bobby resented the time I spent practicing." She laughed bitterly. "How's that for a reversal?"

"I've always wished I could play," Elissa said enthusiastically, glancing at King's set, solemn face and hoping to alleviate the tension Bess's comments were feeding.

"You design clothes, don't you?" the other woman asked curiously, her eyes faintly approving the jump suit. "Did you design that?"

"Yes, do you like it?" Elissa asked eagerly. "I haven't shown this one to my parents. They'd be—" She stopped short, jamming on verbal brakes as King glared at her. "They'd be delighted," she concluded weakly.

"Of course they would. They're very proud of you," King said quickly.

"What do your parents do?" Bess asked politely, raising her glass to her lips.

Elissa gnawed her lip. "They're...they're into ancient history," she said truthfully. Wasn't the Bible a record of human history, after all?

"How interesting." Bess finished her drink, tossing back her hair as she glanced at the diamond-studded watch on her slender wrist. "Bobby's late," she muttered. "Another business meeting that ran overtime. Or so he swears," she added under her breath. "Too bad I'm not a briefcase; I'd be swamped with affection these days."

"It's a difficult time, Bess. Subcontracting can be extremely time-consuming," King reminded her. "Jamaica desperately needs outside investments, and the hotel Bobby's planning will employ a lot of people, help the economy. But it has to be properly built. These things take time."

"It's been months already," Bess muttered dispiritedly.

"It will be over soon," King said, "and you'll be back in Oklahoma City."

Bess looked up. "Yes, I suppose I will. What a trip to look forward to. Instead of staring at hotel walls, I can stare at my own for a change," she said dully. Her eyes searched King's. "You never visit us anymore, Kingston. You spend most of your life here."

King swirled the Scotch in his glass and stuck his free hand into his pocket. "I like Jamaica," he said. He glanced deliberately at Elissa. "A lot."

Bess took an audible breath and drained her glass. "Pour me another, would you, please?" she asked, handing it to King.

"I think you've had enough, Bess," he replied. He took the glass and put it aside, gazing down at a chastened-looking Bess. She merely folded her hands in her lap and looked defeated.

Elissa was trying to decide what to do to cheer them all up when a car came up the winding sandy drive from the main road. A horn sounded, and seconds later, a car door slammed.

"It's Bobby," Bess said dully.

King strode to the door to meet him, and Elissa found Bess staring after him with quiet misery in her eyes.

Elissa watched Bess watching King. "What's your husband like?" she asked, diverting her.

Bess blinked, looking startled. "Bobby? He's...he's a businessman. He doesn't look much like Kingston, even though they had the same mother. Kingston's father was Indian," she added.

"Yes, I know." Elissa smiled at her. "You're very pretty."

Bess's eyes widened. "You're very frank."

"It saves thinking up lies." She cocked her head at the other woman. "How did you and Bobby meet?" she asked.

Bess laughed softly. "You're so unexpected! Bobby was our star quarterback, and I was a cheerleader."

"King says you've been married about ten years, yet you never had children," Elissa mused aloud. "Didn't you want any?"

Bess sighed, looking at her shoes. "When would Bobby ever have time? He's always at the office or on the phone." She pushed back her hair angrily. "I never thought it would be like this. I thought— Anyway, who wants kids?" she murmured, avoiding Elissa's eyes. She shifted restlessly on the couch. "They just clutter up people's lives. I would love to go back to studying piano again, though. But my practicing would disturb Bobby when he's trying to work at home."

"How sad," Elissa said, and meant it. "I think a woman needs fulfillment as a person, just as a man does."

Bess frowned. "It floored me when you asked if I did anything. You know, I never realized that I might be able to do something with myself...."

Elissa heard male voices; King and Bobby were approaching, much to her relief. She was finding this hard going. It shouldn't have bothered her that King was in danger of falling in love with this bitter, confused woman, but it did. It bothered her a lot.

"How long have you and Kingston been...been together?" Bess tried to sound casual, but there was pain in her voice.

"Well..." It was extremely difficult for her to fabricate, and Elissa was grateful that King and a shorter man suddenly appeared in the doorway.

"There you are. Finally," Bess said as the younger man came in a step ahead of King. She looked at him and then averted her eyes. "Did you get what you went for?" she asked. The question sounded innocent enough, but Elissa sensed something in the blonde's voice, something faintly accusing. Perhaps she wondered if Bobby's "business" was really business.

"Of course," Bobby replied. He gave his wife an intent appraisal, his gaze both searching and faintly defensive.

He wasn't anything like King, Elissa decided. His hair was dark blond, and he was blue eyed. He wasn't a bad-looking man at all, and he was slim but well built. He had a nice mouth, and he seemed pleasant enough altogether. But he looked weary and worn, and there were deep lines in his face.

"Your husband has approved the subcontractors," King announced with a grin. "And the bids were well under budget. He'll make you a rich woman yet, Bess."

"How lovely," she said carelessly. "I'll run right out and buy a new mink."

"You'd better get a strong cage and some thick gloves," Elissa said with a mischievous smile.

Bess looked up, clearly puzzled by the remark. She frowned. "Cage? Gloves?"

Bobby got the joke and burst out laughing, instantly looking years younger and more approachable. "I'm afraid you've got it wrong," he told Elissa. "She doesn't want a mink kit. She wants the real thing—a ready-made coat."

"Oh, a fast-food mink in a manner of speaking," Elissa agreed. "Got you."

King's eyes sparkled as he watched her, his firm lips tugging up in a smile. "Watch this girl," he cautioned his half brother. "She's got a quicker mind than I have."

"That'll be the day you old—I mean, darling," she drawled at King, winking. "I happen to know that yours is a genuine steel trap, always set and ready for business."

"A better description I haven't heard," Bobby agreed. "You must be Elissa. Kingston's told me so much about you over the past couple of years that I feel as if I know you already. Tell me, how in the world do you put up with him?"

"Why, there's nothing to it," Elissa said, glancing wickedly at King, and oddly pleased to hear that he talked about her at home. "I got commando training by watching that television show about professional mercenaries."

"I guess that's telling you," Bobby said with a chuckle, winking at King.

"I guess it is," she agreed.

"Kingston isn't all that bad, surely," Bess interrupted, smiling gently up at him. "He's kept me from vegetating on this island for the past two weeks. I don't know how I'd have managed without him."

Bobby laughed, failing to see Bess's intent look at his brother. He seemed to be too busy looking at Elissa. "Good thing, too, considering how little free time I've had," he tossed off to his wife. "You know, Elissa, you're every bit as delightful as Kingston said you were," he added.

Elissa smiled, murmuring a polite reply. She was totally unprepared for the shock and sudden irritation in Bess's eyes.

Three

Bobby spared Bess a faintly curious glance before his attention went back to Elissa. "I'm glad you're back," he told her. "Kingston's been a royal pain these past few days."

King frowned, but he didn't rise to the bait.

"So you did miss me." Elissa batted her lashes at King. "How nice!"

"Of course I missed you," he said curtly. "Bobby, what will you have to drink?"

"Nothing," Bess said quietly. "I'd like to go back to the hotel now," she told her husband with a cool stare. "I'm tired."

"Try sitting in a board meeting for four straight hours and see how relaxed *that* leaves you," her husband challenged. "Look, Bess, we're leaving tomorrow, and I may not see Kingston again for weeks. I want to talk over a new project with him."

"You can use the phone, can't you?" Bess asked, exasperated, as she got gracefully to her feet. In three-inch heels, she was almost her husband's height. "Lord knows you find time to talk to everyone else, but heaven forbid it should be me. Maybe I should make an appointment."

"You just don't understand, do you?" her husband said with a resigned sigh. "Never mind, babe. We'll go." He glanced apologetically at King and Elissa. "Thanks for the invitation, even if I don't get the drink. I'll call you in the morning, big brother."

"Fine," King replied.

"We could go for a ride," Bess murmured to Bobby as he joined her.

"A ride? Are you crazy? I still have to go over bids!" Bobby snapped.

Bess started to speak, then seemed to give up. "Yes, of course." She led the way to the door, calling over her shoulder, "Good night, Kingston, Elissa." She didn't look at either of them. She just kept walking out into the sultry evening breeze.

"I don't know what in hell's gotten into her," Bobby apologized. "She's been worse since we came down here. I can't very well stop working, can I? I don't have time to entertain her; the oil market is too depressed to support us. If we hadn't diversified a few years back into real estate, we'd be living in public housing by now!" He glanced at King. "She's so bored with everything lately. Suppose I let her stay with you for a week or so while I fly back to Oklahoma and catch up at the office?" he asked King in all innocence.

Elissa, standing at the door beside King, could feel him tense against her. "Elissa and I are going to spend a few days with her people in Florida," he replied unexpectedly, his quick glance daring Elissa to deny it. "Not that Bess isn't welcome to use the house..."

"No, I don't want her here alone." Bobby sighed. "It was just a thought. So your people live in Florida?" he added, smiling at Elissa.

"Yes, in Miami," she replied. This was unexpected. Surely King was hedging, but the thought of taking him home with her made her nervous. Her parents didn't approve of her fashions; they certainly weren't going to approve of her friendship with a man like King. They'd think he was a playboy. And for King to actually spend time around her eccentric parents! Her heart almost stopped. But then she reminded herself that he was only playing for time, of course. He wasn't serious.

"What do they do?" Bobby persisted.

"My father is a min—" She caught it just in time, even before King unobtrusively pinched her. She jumped. "He's in ancient history," she bit off, glaring at King. "And my mother is a housewife."

Bobby nodded. "Any brothers or sisters?"

She shook her head gladly. "No. Just me."

"You'd better get going," King interrupted, as if he didn't like the interest Bobby was showing in her. "Bess will take the car if you don't."

"She will at that," he agreed. "Well, good night."

"Good night," King replied.

Bobby left, and a minute later the car roared angrily down the driveway.

"They don't seem ideally suited, do they?" Elissa asked quietly, watching the taillights disappear among the palms.

"They used to be," King replied. "When times were hard, they were always together, doing simple things like window-shopping or just walking. Then, when the money started coming in, Bess was like a kid in a candy shop. She had to have all kinds of expensive things." He sighed. "And Bobby wanted her to have them. He worked harder and harder to give them to her, but it kept him away from home a lot. When the oil market fell, he went into partnership in a small construction firm back home."

He paused, as if thinking, then continued pensively, "Bobby's always felt obliged to compete with me. In recent years, he's tried even harder. That means Bess spends too much time alone, and she isn't the kind of woman who can just sit. She isn't even domestic. Too bad she and Bobby never wanted children."

He turned, missing Elissa's sharp glance. Didn't he know that Bess was just hiding what she really wanted? Elissa was sure that the other woman did want children, very much. He poured himself another Scotch. "Want another?" he asked as an afterthought.

She nodded. "Yes, thanks. Why does he want to compete with you?"

"It's the way he's made, I guess. The second brother isn't going to be second best. He's twenty-eight now, and I think he wants to best me financially before he gets to be my age." He poured Elissa's drink before he opened the sliding doors to the beach. He stood there, tall and unapproachable, the breeze running like fingers through his thick black hair as he watched the surf crash white and frothy onto the hard-packed sand beyond the patio. "He doesn't like the fact that his father allowed me to inherit," he added. "His father and I got along pretty well—in a business sense at least—and I think Bobby somehow felt threatened by that."

"He's your half brother, of course," she said hesitantly, remembering how little King liked to talk about personal matters.

"That's right." He lifted his glass to his lips with a bitter smile. "He's not a duke's mixture—didn't you notice?"

She glared at him. "Neither are you," she snapped. "You're part Apache, which is something else entirely."

He cocked an amused eyebrow at her. "Thank you for clarifying the situation for me," he murmured dryly, and he went back to contemplating the outside world.

For a few minutes they sipped their drinks in silence, and Elissa wondered at the sense of freedom the liquor gave her. She hadn't had more than a small glass of wine in a long time. But the vodka seemed to be doing strange things to her, making her extremely aware of King, diluting her inhibitions. She felt light-headed. Reckless. Her body burned with new temptations. She put down the empty glass, and her hand seemed to move in slow motion. King was close to finishing his drink, too. Was it his third? She couldn't keep track. Bess had gotten to him, all right. Elissa wondered if he was completely sober.

"Do you have other family?" she asked after a minute, joining him in the doorway.

"Bobby's father died some years back. Our mother is in a nursing home," he added simply. "Alzheimer's disease. We visit her, but she doesn't know us anymore."

"How terrible for you. And for her."

"It is that," he agreed. He took a long swallow. "I don't know about my own father. He got sick of my mother's rich friends and left us when I was just a boy." He studied his glass. "He was from New Mexico, but he worked on oil rigs in Oklahoma. That's where he met my mother." He glanced at her. "She was blond and blue eyed, like Bobby, and she loved the good life. Money was everything to her. My father had simpler tastes."

"I wouldn't have asked," she replied quietly. It startled her that he was willing to share such a personal thing with her. Either he was extremely upset by Bess, or the alcohol was affecting him.

She stared at his shirt where he'd unbuttoned it and removed his tie. Against the white fabric, his skin looked even darker than usual. Her eyes were drawn to the thick mesh of hair over hard, bronzed muscle.

As if he sensed that rapt stare, he turned toward her and his eyes caught hers. He didn't look away. While her heart went wild, with deliberate slowness he tossed away the cigarette he'd just lit and took a step toward her, bringing her totally against him, so that her breasts touched his chest where his shirt was open. She wasn't wearing anything under the jump suit, and she could feel her nipples harden at the contact with him. Tensing away from him, she wondered uncomfortably if he felt them, too.

"Anything sexual disturbs you, doesn't it?" he asked softly, well aware of the tension in her body. "Well, I'm safe—you said so yourself. So why don't you cut your teeth on me?"

"I can't!" she gasped. He had her with her back to the sliding glass door, so that she was trapped between its coldness and his warmth, her breasts wildly sensitive against his hard chest.

"Shh," he whispered at her temple. "Don't panic. I won't hurt you." He smiled softly. The drinks had done the trick; he was finally feeling relaxed and slightly muddled, which was a relief from all the heavy thinking he'd had to do lately. He couldn't have Bess, he reasoned now, but Elissa was fair game, wasn't she? Shy and virginal—how tempting to a man. What would it hurt to give her a little experience? He cared about her, in a way. And who better to deal with her repressions? She'd almost admitted earlier that she'd let him.

"Why are you doing this?" she asked in a high-pitched tone. Her fingers started to push him away, but when her hands encountered warm, hair-roughened skin, they stopped struggling and flattened against him. She realized she didn't feel like resisting, anyway. The vodka had done something to her willpower. She felt more like relaxing against King than fighting him; his proximity was having a throbbing effect on her body.

"Because I need something to occupy me, to keep me out of trouble. So you're going to be my hobby," he said.

"I don't want to be your hobby," she protested weakly. Her legs felt trembly.

"I was yours at the beginning," he reminded her. "You've no one to blame but yourself."

"That was different. You were repressed," she said defensively. He was too close. She was inhaling the tangy, clean scent of him, and it was intoxicating her more than the vodka had. His bared chest was hard under her fingers, and between seeing him and smelling him and feeling him, she was adrift on sensation, her heart pounding. All that devastating masculinity, so close.

"*I* was repressed?" he asked with an amused smile.

"You were all alone," she said quietly, avoiding his eyes. "I felt sorry for you. I was alone, too. I ... well, I thought it would be nice to have a friend."

"You had Warchief," he pointed out, grinning. "Speaking of Warchief..." He glanced around. The big parrot was on his perch ring, one foot drawn up, his eyes closed. "Unusual, his going to sleep without being covered. Is that antibiotic working, do you think?"

"He isn't sneezing or rasping," she said, grateful for the change of subject. "He's better. He's just sleepy. He always goes to sleep at dusk, when you're not around." She grinned. "He's in love with you."

"I think he's a she," he laughed. Then he turned his attention back to her, looking down at the bodice of her jump suit with narrowing eyes. He moved experimentally, rubbing his chest against her, and she gasped at the sudden, sharp pleasure the friction produced.

She flushed to the roots of her long dark hair. "King!"

"Shocking, isn't it?" he asked, lifting his narrow gaze to hers.

Her eyes searched his, curiosity momentarily displacing her nervousness at this new intimacy.

His gaze held hers while the hands at her waist began to move her in a sensuous circle against his hard, warm chest.

The only sounds she heard were the hoarseness of the ocean against the sand and the wildness of her own breathing. She couldn't bear to look at King as sensation overwhelmed her, and she lowered her forehead to his shoulder. He was breathing heavily, too, his heartbeat audible.

His thumbs edged under her arms, brushing at the sides of her breasts, feeling her softness, feeling her begin to tremble with the newness of physical pleasure.

"You aren't wearing a bra, are you?" he whispered, his voice deep and soft at her ear. "That silky thing is so thin that it's like holding you naked in my arms."

The power of the erotic suggestion was such that Elissa bit her lip to keep from crying out. Her nails dug into his shoulders, and her legs threatened to buckle underneath her. She shuddered.

"Elissa," he breathed roughly.

She could smell the Scotch on his breath, but even that was oddly exciting. His arms suddenly lifted her into an embrace tight enough that she could feel his ribs digging into her. She clung to him, her face buried in his throat, breathing in the exquisitely male scent of him, her head spinning, her body aching for something it had never known, her breasts crushed against hard muscle. He bit her ear, then ran his tongue around its soft curves, an intimate gesture that she'd never realized could have such a profound effect.

Her arms tightened around his neck, her face fiery with unexpected passion as he held her. Was she mistaken, or was there a fine tremor in the arms so fiercely holding her?

His cheek brushed against hers. "Your breasts feel swollen," he whispered, once more moving her body against him. "Do they ache?" he whispered knowingly.

"Yes," she gasped mindlessly. "Oh, King!" Her curiosity outweighed her caution, outweighed the fear that had always come with the threat of intimacy, and she reveled in the feel of his slick, damp skin against her tender breasts.

"I can make them stop aching," he whispered huskily. His lips traveled down her face to her throat, his breathing harsh and rapid. "Here..."

His mouth slid over the silky bodice and suddenly pressed, open and hot, right against the soft curve of her thinly veiled breast.

She cried out at the pleasure it gave her, and her back arched to give him access.

But the sound had shocked King into realizing what he was doing. His head jerked up, his eyes wide and frankly stunned. "Dear God," he said harshly. He hadn't expected this. Hadn't expected to want her. He hadn't known it until now, hadn't dreamed... He felt the tautness of his body and suddenly released her and turned away, not wanting her to know what she was doing to him.

She gaped at him. He was breathing harshly as he reached over to pick up his nearly finished drink from the table. His hand seemed to tremble a little as he lifted the glass to his mouth and drained it. "I'm sorry," he bit off, setting the glass down hard on the table. "I didn't expect that to happen."

He was apologizing, she registered, but for what? For wanting her? "I don't...mind." She said it and was amazed to find that it was true. She didn't mind having him want her. It was heady and wildly exciting.

He turned, his dark eyes glazed and questioning. "Why not?"

She shrugged helplessly. "I don't know." Her eyes fell to his chest. "I still ... I still ache," she whispered shakily.

His lips were parted, as if he was finding it difficult to breathe. "Have you felt like that with anyone else?" he asked, distressed to realize it was suddenly deeply important that he know.

"No," she confessed, her voice soft, gentle.

He couldn't decide what to do. Should he send her home or pick her up in his arms and take her into his bed and show her how sweet he could make it for her? Damn. How could just a couple of drinks make him so addled?

She looked up at that moment and saw the indecision in his eyes, and she knew exactly what had caused it. Her face colored. "I—I can't sleep with you," she whispered huskily. "I . . . like what you just did to me, but . . . I can't deal with that kind of easy intimacy. Not even with you."

His dark eyes roamed down her body, the sight of that sweet softness he'd known so briefly making him ache. He caught her eyes. "I can make you want it," he said in a stranger's sensuous voice.

"And after?" she asked.

He drew in a slow breath. "My God, what am I saying?"

"It's been a hard night for you," she said, forcing herself not to take it too seriously. He was frustrated, that was all, and she was handy and he'd forgotten all the reasons why not. "I wish things were different."

"So do I." He rammed his hands into his pockets. "Believe me, so do I." It was the truth, his body fairly throbbed with wanting her. How odd, his muddled brain mused, to have this kind of reaction to Elissa when it was Bess he'd been afraid of wanting. Could it be misplaced desire? Lord, he couldn't even think straight.

"I'd better go home."

He turned. "I'll walk you."

"No. It's all right. You can watch me out the door," she said quickly—too quickly.

"I can't help it, you know," he said softly, accurately reading the apprehension in her lovely face and smiling in spite of himself when she colored. "A man's body will give him away every time. But I trust you not to take advantage of it," he added with dry humor.

She stared at him, then gasped with helpless laughter, "You horrible man!"

"Well, I'm vulnerable," he commented as he opened the front door and stood aside to let her pass. "A man has to look out for his honor, after all. I might marry someday. She'll want to be the first."

"I'm sure she'd be at least the fifteenth," she chided, laughing at her own boldness. Now that the heart-shattering truth of just moments before had passed, it was once again easy to talk to him, even about the intimate things.

"Not quite that many," he mumbled as they walked, the breeze, warm and salty smelling, ruffling the fronds of the palm trees.

"Well, you didn't learn what you did back there by reading a book," she observed.

He cocked an eyebrow and laughed faintly. "No, I didn't." He stopped, tilting her chin up. "God, it was sweet."

Her lips parted, and her breath caught in her throat. Then he laughed softly, angrily, as he took her arm, almost roughly, and propelled her along the moonlit beach. "I must be drunk," he muttered. "You'll have to overlook a few things about tonight, I guess. I haven't been myself."

Which was absolutely true. Even speaking was hard for him right now. He needed a cold shower—badly. And for some reason, he didn't want Elissa to know what he was feeling, to know the extent of this bizarre aberration in his thought processes. It shocked him, the sudden hunger he felt to strip her out of that jump suit, throw her down on the beach and make her his. He remembered how she'd looked in that sexy nightgown, and he almost groaned out loud. He had to be drunk all right, he told himself. How could he even imagine a union between them? She with her hang-ups and he with his impossibly confused feelings for Bess. Was this what people meant by love on the rebound? Or had he always wanted Elissa and refused to acknowledge it in the face of her physical reticence?

"You're very quiet," she said when they reached her door.

"I'm shocked at my own behavior," he said curtly.

"It's been difficult for you," she returned, unable to meet his eyes. "It was just the alcohol."

"Yes. It must have been. We'll forget it happened."

"That might be best," she said lightly, forcing herself not to show the disquiet she felt.

"You don't need to make it sound so damned easy," he said, unreasonably irritated and finding himself on the verge of spewing out exactly what he'd wanted to keep silent about, yet unable to stop himself. His self-control was shot. "Do you know how much I want to lay you down in the sand and have you? Do you?" he demanded harshly. "And because of that, you'd better stay away from me until I get myself together." Hurting, and lashing out because of it, he straightened to deal the killing blow. "Because anything I did right now would be because of Bess—wanting Bess—and you'd better remember it."

It was a lie—he was too confused to know his own mind right now—but he reasoned that enough people stood to get hurt by Bess's recent interest in him, and he didn't want Elissa to become a casualty, too. Anything—anything at all—that would keep her at arm's length would ultimately be for her own good. She didn't need to compromise her innocence because of his confused longings. So he'd have to be cruel to be kind, even though she wouldn't realize it right now. Someday, however, she'd thank him for what must seem like callous behavior.

She clenched her teeth. He hadn't exactly shocked her with the admission—she'd suspected she'd been a stand-in for Bess—but had he needed to be so blunt? "Then I'll say good night."

"Say it, and go inside." He jammed his hands into his pockets.

"What a sweet-tempered man you are," she muttered. She turned to unlock the door, then glared at him over her shoulder as she went inside. "Thanks for a lovely evening. I did so enjoy it."

He glared back. "Including the way you threw yourself at me back there?" he asked with a cold, mocking smile, pushing her that last step.

He was asking for a hard slap. She tried to remember that he'd been drinking, but all she wanted to do was push him into a coral reef and whistle for a passing shark! "I was drinking," she admitted, "and so were you."

"Well, I won't make the same mistake with you again," he returned coldly. "Obviously you can't hold your liquor." He didn't know why he was goading her—why didn't he let her go inside, where she'd be safely away from him?

"Said the pot to the kettle!" she threw back, fuming. "You were the one who started it!"

"You weren't fighting very hard," he pointed out.

She clenched her fists. "Next time you need help with your love life, find another pigeon. I'm not playing second fiddle to you and your sister-in-law!"

"Stop shouting," he grumbled.

"I'll shout if I like. And I want my bird back!"

"When he's well, with my blessing," he shot back.

Her lower lip trembled. She was near tears. With her fists clenched at her sides, she felt herself shaking with mingled rage and frustration. Here she was yelling things she didn't mean but couldn't help saying, and she didn't know what to do about it. She'd never felt like this before, and she didn't even understand what was wrong.

"I hate you!" she wailed.

He took his hands out of his pockets and moved close, cupping her head in his lean fingers, holding her firmly. "Do you, Elissa?" That's what he'd wanted, wasn't it? To protect her from himself? But as he gazed down into her wide, glistening eyes, he felt a wave of emotion crash over him, engulfing him in frustrated desire. He was only human, after all.

"In lieu of a cold shower..." he said under his breath, and he bent his head.

Elissa's mouth felt bruised from the sheer force of his hard lips, and he didn't spare her. His mouth lifted for an instant, only to come down again more intimately, his tongue pushing into her mouth, his fingers biting into her to tilt her head and give him better access to her lips.

She moaned, and he caught his breath. "Open your mouth," he ground out, his hands at her throat, lifting, coaxing. "Oh, God, Elissa, open your mouth. . . ."

She did, shuddering as he deepened the kiss. Her knees weakened and threatened to collapse, but the instant her body relaxed against the rigid strength of his, he seemed to come to his senses. His lips lifted slowly, delicately probing, brushing. He felt her breasts, so smooth and hard tipped, press against him, saw her expression soft with confused desire. Elissa. He blinked, his mind in limbo. He wanted her. His body ached to have hers, to press it into the soft sand beneath his, to feel her skin warm and welcoming under his hands. . . .

Elissa. . . He cursed under his breath and stopped abruptly, feeling outraged at his lack of control. He hadn't meant for this to happen. That damned Scotch! What was he doing? He went rigid and suddenly all but threw her away from him.

"Was that what you wanted?" he demanded, wanting to hurt, to make her pay for that lapse in his control. "Now you know, so go inside, little girl. You'll have to get the rest of your experience with someone else. I don't initiate virgins."

She swallowed. He wasn't making any sense at all; he was being totally erratic. His fists clenched, and she saw the shudder ripple through his powerful body. Too much to drink, her mind registered. Dangerous.

"Who asked you to?" she shot back. She hated him. She hated him! With shaking hands she opened the door, went inside and slammed it behind her, locking it, as well. Outside she heard a harsh muttered curse.

She collapsed against the wall with an unsteady sigh. She hadn't expected that. As a matter of fact, about the *last* thing she'd expected after his outburst was for him to kiss her. He'd never kissed her before tonight. Come to think of it, they'd never argued before. She felt a lump in her throat as she realized that she'd just lost a good friend and she didn't even understand why.

His footsteps died away, and all she heard was the gentle wind off the Caribbean. She touched her lips, feeling their swollen fullness with wonder. Her tongue touched them and tasted him.

It all seemed like a dream. For some reason King had stepped completely out of character, and for that matter, she had, too. But none of it made any sense. Surely if King were pining away for his sister-in-law, he wouldn't be capable of that kind of passion with another woman. Or would he? She cursed her ignorance of men and their basic makeup.

Trying to sort things out, she concluded that if King needed to used her as a shield, he must have some kind of special feeling for Bess. The tender look in his eyes when he'd gazed at his sister-in-law had afforded Elissa a rare glimpse behind the mask of cool reserve King usually wore. Apparently, Bess had always been special to him, and now, maybe for the first time, he was confronting her in a new way—as a desirable woman, not just as a relative.

Elissa sighed, remembering with guilt her own delicious abandon in King's arms. She was sure the drinks had influenced her. They'd obviously influenced him, too. She went into her bedroom and flicked on the light, quietly removing the jump suit and putting on a long, plain cotton nightgown. King had reminded her that anything he did to her would be only out of desire for Bess. Was that completely true? she wondered. There were so many puzzles now. Their uncomplicated friendship had turned into a mental wrestling match.

She brushed her long hair and crawled into bed. But once she turned out the light, she could feel all over again the warmth of King's lips on hers, his tongue pushing into her mouth in a kiss unlike any she'd ever experienced. She felt her face go hot as she remembered just how involved he'd gotten. And he'd accused *her* of throwing herself at *him*! Incredible, how much his sharp words had hurt. Of course, she'd been spared his temper for the past two years. She might never have seen it if he hadn't made such a blatant pass at her in the first place. Men!

Well, her sexy nightie was still lying on his bed, she remembered; she hoped it gave him nightmares. She rolled over and closed her eyes, counting waves and praying for sleep. You can just hold your breath until I do you another favor, King Roper, she thought furiously.

Four

In her wild and confusing dreams, Elissa felt King's hands caressing her, molding her curves, teaching her new movements, new sensations. She could see his face taut with passion, feel the ripple of his muscles as he began a pagan rhythm with his body....

She sat up straight in bed, drenched with sweat and trembling from the effects of those sensuous and disturbing dreams. Her own reactions shocked her. Were all those years of suppressing her sensuality about to explode in her face? Last night her old fears of intimacy had dropped away, and she'd felt straightforward desire for the first time in her life.

It was the vodka, she thought stubbornly, trying desperately to get her delinquent emotions under control. After all, how could she forget that King had accused her of throwing herself at him?

"Sure I did," she muttered as she went into the living room that overlooked the beach. "Sure I did. I forced him to hold me like that and kiss my..."

She swallowed, ignoring the instant hardening of her nipples. This was outrageous! Where was her pride?

She made herself a cup of coffee and opened a packaged pastry, nibbling at it halfheartedly as she began to scribble ideas for new designs on her big sketch pad. Unfortunately, nothing appealed to her. She stayed with her work for a few minutes and then gave up, walking out onto her small patio. Her long hair and wildly colorful caftan fluttered in the eternal breeze from the sea, and she let the sound of the surf soothe her as she gazed appreciatively at a big sailboat on the horizon.

Jamaica was the stuff of dreams, she mused. Pirate legends and fascinating people. Her eyes turned toward a distant hill, at the top of which the structure called Rose Hall perched. If legend was fact, its long-ago owner, Annee Palmer, whom the locals had dubbed the White Witch of Rose Hall, had murdered three husbands and several lovers there, in addition to practicing voodoo and brutalizing her slaves.

Once, after a tour of the spooky house, Elissa had had nightmares for days. One night, she recalled, she'd awakened screaming, and she'd heard a pounding at her door. King, his pajama bottoms peeking out above the waistband of his trousers testifying to his haste in rushing to her cottage, had, upon assessing that nothing was wrong, laughed at her indulgently and cradled her like a child. Even then, she reflected, sitting on the edge of her bed and holding her, he hadn't seemed to notice her as a woman. There had been nothing remotely sexual about the comfort he'd given her. And yet now, after last night, it was impossible to think of him in a nonsexual way.

She stepped down onto the beach and saw that King's car was gone. Where was he? she wondered briefly. Deciding it was really none of her business, she brushed back her hair and turned once again to watch the big passenger ship in the distance wend its way seaward. Her cottage was too far off the beaten track for much contact with city life, and she liked it that way. All the same, it must be fascinating to live in Mo' Bay, as everyone called Montego Bay, and see the people who visited the island from those grand oceangoing hotels.

With her coffee cup in her hands, she sat down on the warm sand and watched the graceful casuarina pines blow in the wind. It was heaven here. So peaceful and quiet and exquisitely unpolluted.

Her eyes drifted closed, and suddenly she envisioned herself on the beach with King, in the moonlight, making wild, passionate love, with the surf crashing around them....

Her eyes popped open, and she jumped to her feet so quickly that she almost upended her coffee all over herself. Dazed by her wayward thoughts, she stumbled back inside and went straight to work. And this time she did three designs that satisfied her creative instincts.

It was the longest day she could remember. At dusk she heard Warchief go off like an air-raid siren and wished that she could get him and bring him home, but it was misting rain and he was better off where he was for the time being. She was feeling unaccountably lonely, and she missed having him on his big T-stand perch in the living room, chattering away and begging scraps when she broke off work for a snack or a meal. She almost always ended up sharing fresh fruits and vegetables and bread, which he ate with evident enjoyment.

She sighed, turning away from the window. She missed her bird. She was going to miss King even more. After last night, she was sure he wouldn't have anything else to do with her. She still found it amazing that he'd wanted to take her to bed. She was glad she'd had the sense to refuse, but she still flushed thinking about what she'd let him do to her by those sliding glass doors. Best to put such errant thoughts out of her mind, she chided herself.

Just after dark, she was puttering around the kitchen in shorts and a long-sleeved man's shirt when she saw King drive up to his villa, accompanied by Bobby and Bess. She frowned. Weren't they supposed to have left that morning?

Minutes later, her phone rang.

"I'm home," King said in a deep, sexy tone that she knew instantly was a ruse. "Why don't you come over and have a drink? Bess and Bobby are staying the night with me."

She fished for excuses. "I have to feed the hermit crabs and put out lobster pots...."

"I'll see you in five minutes," he said, ignoring her feeble attempt at humor, and hung up.

She glared at the telephone. She wanted to call him back and tell him what he could do with his overbearing attitude, but now that she'd begun this horrible charade, she felt obliged to go through with it. Why, she didn't know.

After changing into a strappy little black dress, hose and high heels, she tramped across to King's house.

Warchief went into raucous ecstasies of welcome at her arrival. "Quiet, sweet thing," Elissa scolded playfully, nodding to Bobby and a subdued Bess as she went to pet her parrot.

Evidently he'd lost his inclination to bite. He blazed his eyes, docilely bent his head for her to scratch and cooed, "Hello, pretty thing."

"I've missed you, too, you horrible bird," she murmured, nuzzling her nose against his head.

"I wouldn't put *my* nose that close to him," Bess gasped.

"Wise decision," King remarked easily. "He's totally unpredictable. He won't let anyone except Elissa that close."

"Now go to sleep," Elissa whispered when she'd scratched his green head enough to satisfy Warchief and his eyes were nearly closed.

She busied herself covering his cage, uneasier around King than she'd ever been in the two years she'd known him. She couldn't even manage to meet his eyes, she was so confused.

"I expected to find you already over here," Bess remarked. Dressed in flowing yellow lounging pajamas that suited her blondness, she leaned back on the big white sofa.

"I had some designs to work on," Elissa replied.

"She works better at her own cottage, where there are fewer distractions," King remarked, his dark eyes narrow on her averted face.

Bobby hadn't said a word, except to greet Elissa warmly. He was bent over financial reports spread all over the coffee table, seemingly oblivious to the world around him.

Bess gave him a weary glance before she turned back to study Elissa and King. "So what's with you two? You barely seem to be speaking," she observed. Her eyes openly flirted with King.

King cleared his throat and stared hard at Elissa. "How astute of you to notice, Bess. Actually, Elissa and I had a little tiff, but it's nothing, really."

"Yes," Elissa began, glaring at him. "I simply lost control and threw myself at—" Suddenly she found herself being grabbed by the hand and dragged into a bedroom.

"Rape!" she yelled, and Bobby surprised everyone by bursting out with laughter.

King closed the door behind them, his face livid. He leaned back against the door, watching her retreat to the window.

"Stop that," he growled. "You're slitting my throat!"

"Good. I'll bet you bleed ice water," she returned, her eyes wide and accusing.

"I shouldn't have said what I said last night," he began slowly. "I'm sorry. I can't begin to explain why I did it."

"You were drunk and so was I," she replied to save face. His eyebrow made an arch. "On three drinks?"

"I'm not used to liquor of any sort," she defended herself. "And unless I'm mistaken, you don't drink much, either."

His powerful shoulders rose and fell. In his white slacks and a red-and-white knit shirt, he looked impossibly handsome. His dark eyes ran up and down her body, and she knew he was remembering, as she had, how it had been between them. Her heart pounded once again at the sheer impact of that memory.

"Bobby postponed his flight until tomorrow morning," he said a few moments later. "He thought it would be fun if the four of us flew back to the States together."

"I can't," she protested. "Warchief—"

"I've got a sitter, as usual," he returned. "I can't stay here or Bess will get a migraine or find some excuse to stay with me. Bobby, as you can see, is immersed in his work. He doesn't even realize what's happening."

"You poor man," she said coolly.

He glared at her. "Do you think I can help it?"

"No," she sighed, turning away. "I don't suppose she can help it, either."

He came up behind her, his warm, strong hands clasping her arms. She trembled at their touch, so aware of him physically that it made her ache.

His fingers contracted rhythmically, as if he liked the silky feel of her skin. His breath in her hair was warm and not quite steady.

"We can fly to Miami, and then I can drive you to your parents' house. That will accomplish two things: satisfy my sense of honesty and get Bess out of my hair."

So he wasn't planning to stay, thank God. But what would her parents say at this unexpected visit? They were bound to wonder why she'd cut her vacation short and why King was with her. This entire situation was totally ludicrous. Yet, despite herself, her heart went out to King in his predicament, and she reasoned it wouldn't hurt her work any to touch base in Florida. Maybe her parents wouldn't have to see King, and they'd never know that anything was amiss.

"All right," she agreed. "I'll go."

"Good girl."

She turned and looked up at him. "Yes, I am," she said quietly. "Try to remember that the next time you decide to make a pass at me."

He searched her soft blue eyes. "You and I are an explosive mixture, aren't we?" he asked, his voice deep and measured.

Her nails were making quiet patterns on his shirtfront while she looked at him. "Until last night, I never really understood why women couldn't stop men from making love to them," she confessed. "It's very hard to stop, isn't it?"

He smiled indulgently. "Well, a woman *can* tease a man until he's desperate to have her."

"I tease sometimes," she admitted slowly, searching his darkening eyes, "but I don't really mean it. Not as a come-on." She lowered her gaze to his throat. "I've always wanted to be more like Bess," she said. "Sophisticated and worldly and very desirable. But the minute a man comes too close, I freeze. All those old inhibitions rear up, and I run. But I don't mean to be cruel. It's . . . like a fantasy."

He tilted her face up to his. "I think I've always known that, Elissa," he said quietly. "And I know you weren't teasing me. Not deliberately, anyway," he added with a smile. "Though you did get a little wild."

She blushed feverishly.

"What I'm trying to explain," he continued, tracing her cheek, "is that I was frustrated and I couldn't do anything about it. I ended up saying a lot of things I didn't mean."

"So did I," she replied. "I—I ached."

"Not half as much as I did," he said with a mock groan. He pushed her long hair away from her face. "I lay awake half the night, picturing you nude, on the beach, your arms open for me,'' he said huskily.

''Why, that's just what I—!'' She stopped, her mouth open, horrified at what she'd admitted.

''There's nothing to be ashamed of,'' he said gently. ''You're human. So am I. We had a little too much to drink, we quarreled—that's all.''

''King, you—you won't try to seduce me?'' she asked, afraid that he might out of frustration over Bess and knowing from last night's experience that he wouldn't meet much resistance.

''Could I?'' he asked in a smooth, sensuous tone, searching her wide eyes.

''Yes,'' she admitted, lowering her gaze.

His own reaction startled him; it was instantaneous and overwhelming, and he caught his breath as his body tautened. He saw her blush scarlet at the awareness of what was happening to him, and he muttered unsteadily, ''This is absurd.''

''King?'' she whispered, her body throbbing wildly from the knowledge of what her response had done to him.

''Oh, what the hell,'' he breathed, and he bent to her mouth.

His lips came down on hers and opened them sensuously, while his arms lifted her against him, savoring her soft weight. He carried her to the huge king-size bed and placed her carefully on the black silk coverlet. Then he slid alongside her, his look lazy, his eyes dangerous. Lowering his head, he trailed a string of warm, moist kisses from her temple to her throat.

''Does this untie?'' he murmured, searching her shoulders for the ends of the straps.

Her lips parted. She thought she wanted to protest, but her body was singing to her, her blood raging in her veins. She wanted his eyes on her, there, his mouth, she wanted...

"You have bedroom eyes," he whispered. His fingers found the tiny bows just behind her shoulders, and he untied them very slowly. "When I look in them I can see what you want."

"What do I want?" she whispered, her voice husky and unfamiliar to her own ears as she lay beneath him.

"My eyes," he replied, drawing the bodice of her dress down just to the soft beginning slope of her breasts. "And my mouth." He bent his head to her creamy skin, running his lips just beneath her collarbone in slow, sensuous sweeps. His hands were on her rib cage, smoothing the black crepe, his thumbs just under her breasts, touching them as if by accident.

Her fists clenched beside her head, and her breath caught. He lifted his head, looking at her.

"You're trembling," he breathed, reaching for the top of the bodice.

"King," she moaned helplessly.

"Innocent," he whispered. He held her eyes as his hands moved, and she felt the cool night air on her breasts as the fabric fell to her waist.

"Oh!" she whispered softly, arching her body gently.

His gaze moved slowly down to her breasts, their small pink nipples aroused and hard, her body shuddering a little with the newness of this kind of intimacy.

"The first time," he said under his breath. "My God, they're exquisite." His lightly callused fingers brushed them, tenderly tracing their contours, touching the hard nipples just lightly enough to make her shudder with pleasure.

She couldn't even speak; her throat was tight with exquisite tension.

"Now," he whispered, bending. "Now, Elissa, now..."

His hand cupped her while his mouth opened on her, and she cried out. Then his mouth caught hers, stifling the tiny sound while his hand possessed her, savoring her silky warmth.

"I could eat you," he ground out against her eager, open mouth. "I could eat you like candy."

Another sound tore from her, and he lifted his head, looking dazedly past her to the radio. His hand trembled as he reached for the volume and turned it on to a heavy reggae beat.

"Now," he murmured, "you can make as much noise as you want."

Her lips opened to voice a protest, and his crushed down over it, his tongue moving into her mouth with a slow, hungry rhythm, his knee easing between her legs.

She felt her fingernails digging into the nape of his neck, reveling in the feel of his thick dark hair. Her body was on fire for him; she'd never in her life felt anything as explosively sexual. She wanted fulfillment; she wanted to be part of him, rock with him, writhe under him.

Her moans grew sharper when his mouth traveled down over her breasts to her waist, her stomach. She moved helplessly in his embrace, feeling his strength, loving his hands, loving the ardor of his warm mouth.

He paused, breathing raggedly, to strip off his shirt, and she gasped at the sight of him like that, looming over her, his chest thick with dark hair, the bronzed muscles rippling, his face dark with passion, his eyes almost black. She could feel the heat of his body, see the fine tremor of his arms.

"Come here," he commanded, kneeling before her.

She rose to her own knees, and he pulled her to him, pressing her breasts hard against his hair-roughened chest and making her shudder with the fierce pleasure of it. He held her there, kissing her deeply and shifting her against him in the process until her nipples were so sensitized that they burned and her nails dug into his back.

"I want...you," was dragged out of her throat. She buried her face in his neck and clung to him, her hips against his, her thighs trembling. "I...want...you."

His hands went to her hips, grinding her into him, and a burning sensation shot through her lower body. She shuddered helplessly, gasping with pleasure and barely contained desire.

"Lie down," he whispered shakily. "Lie down under me. I'll make you stop shaking. I'll make you part of me...."

"The door...is it locked?" she asked huskily, feeling his weight come over her, his hands urgent on her body.

"Locked?" His hands stilled, and he looked into her feverish eyes. "Elissa?" He swallowed, his bare chest rising and falling with the force of his heartbeat as he looked down at her. "Elissa...I could make you pregnant."

She was hardly able to breathe. His eyes were the world. She loved him, and she hadn't known. He was more than her friend. He was everything. And to have his child—the thought was too wonderful for words.

Her eyes went down his body possessively, loving its long, powerful lines, loving every inch of him with sweet abandon. Her hips moved sensuously under his, eliciting a groan from him.

"No, honey," he whispered, stilling her impatient movements. "Don't make me. We've got to stop while we can."

"Why?" she asked dazedly.

"We can't make love with Bobby and Bess sitting in the next room." He laughed brittlely. "I must have been out of my mind to let things go this far."

His hands cupped her head, and he dropped a hard, quick kiss onto her lips. Then he sat up, smoothing his hands blatantly over her breasts, his eyes appreciative and boldly possessive. "God, you're something," he said. "As hot and wild as I am. We'd set fires together," he added with what sounded like regret.

She sat up, too, more than unsettled by the confusing sequence of events and moods. Feeling uncomfortably exposed beneath that frank stare of his, she tugged at her bodice, but his hand prevented her from tugging it up.

"Not yet," he murmured. His hand went to her back, arching her over his arm, and his mouth opened, taking her breast inside the moist darkness.

She shuddered, biting her lip to keep from crying out. It was the sweetest kind of ache he made there, his tongue rubbing lazily at her nipple, his lips tugging at her. She clutched the back of his dark head, holding him there, while his free hand came up just below his mouth and cupped her sensuously.

It was a long time before he lifted his head, and he clearly liked what he saw when he looked at her. "I'd like to have you on the beach, just the way I dreamed of."

She flushed to the roots of her hair at the image that had haunted her all day, too.

His hand moved over her soft breasts. "You're very pale here," he said. "I'd like to teach you the delicious pleasure of sunbathing nude. Swimming nude."

"You do," she said without thinking, her voice breathless sounding.

He lifted his head, smiling slowly. "Yes. You've watched me sometimes at night, from your kitchen window, haven't you?"

The flush got worse, but she didn't look away. "I was curious," she confessed softly. "There was moonlight once, and you came out of the water very close to the cottage . . . I never knew a man could be beautiful." She faltered, blushing furiously. "I didn't think you'd know I was watching."

He brushed his mouth over her eyes. "I knew," he murmured. "I don't mind if you look at me."

She was still trembling when he got to his feet and pulled her up with him, slowly retying the straps at her shoulders.

"You look loved," he said unexpectedly. He brushed her tangled hair away from her damp face, then turned away to pick up his shirt.

To Elissa's amazement, her hand reached out to protest when he started to put it on.

He looked up in surprise, then gently drew her hands to him. "Go ahead. Indulge yourself."

"You don't mind?" she asked, savoring his hair-roughened skin with hands that had never known a man's body.

"Mind? Not in the least," he returned. "Come here. I'll teach you how."

She hadn't known there was a right and wrong way to touch a man, but with his hands showing her how, urging her mouth to his skin, teaching her what excited him, what pleased him the most, she felt her confidence grow, and with it a new sense of womanly power. She didn't protest, not even when he guided her hands and let her experience him in a way she'd never dreamed of.

Finally he emitted a low groan and slid her arms around his waist.

"Sometimes I forget how innocent you are," he said in her ear. He bit it, laughing softly, and his cheek nuzzled hers. "You make me forget," he whispered. He drew his mouth across her cheek, then raised his head to search her eyes. "You shut out the world while I'm holding you."

He kissed her gently then, and she understood. She blotted out his hunger for Bess—that was what he meant.

But I love you, she wanted to say. I love you, and I want so much more of you than this. Two years of friendship, and it had never occurred to her just how necessary he'd become to her, just how possessive she'd become of him. Nothing he'd done to her was unwelcome. She realized she could lie with him and give herself and live on it for the rest of her life, despite all her hard-won principles. Was that lust? Or was it the natural hunger for oneness, for total knowledge?

With his mouth still over hers, she frowned and opened her eyes, only to find his eyes open and watching her. Her heart went wild. His tongue penetrated her mouth, his hands came up under her breasts, and she couldn't sustain the look a second longer. She closed her eyes with a hungry moan, and he kissed her deeply, thoroughly, before finally releasing her and putting her from him. She straightened up and smoothed out her dress as best she could.

"Don't brush your hair," he said when she reached for a brush on his dresser just as they were about to leave the room.

"Why not? I must look a mess."

"Because I want her to see you like this," he said gruffly. "With your mouth swollen and your hair in a tangle and your skin glowing. I want her to know that we've been making love."

"That's cruel," she whispered.

"I have to be cruel, don't you see? My God, Elissa, he's my brother," he groaned.

"Yes, I know." She stood in front of him, reaching up to smooth away his frown. She smiled gently, drowning in new fantasies, brimming over with her new knowledge of him, new memories to put under her pillow and cherish.

"Too bad you're such an innocent," he said with a sigh.

"What would you do if I weren't?" she teased gently.

"I'd take you into my bed and work Bess out of my system with a vengeance," he said honestly. "And I could, with you. I've never wanted anyone so much in all my life."

"I wish I could let you," she replied. "I think I'd like sleeping with you, King. Lovemaking is more beautiful than I ever realized."

"I'm glad you think of it that way, and not as something to satisfy a passing physical urge," he said. "Ideally it is an act of love. With you," he added quietly, bemusedly, "it feels like it. I don't understand...."

She drew in a slow breath and went to turn the radio off, flushing at the reason it had been turned on. She looked across the room and found him watching her.

"There's no need to blush," he said quietly, once again reading her mind. "You did my ego a world of good—believe me. If it hadn't been for our houseguests, I wouldn't have given a damn if you'd yelled the place down."

"It's embarrassing to feel like this," she whispered. "They'll see...."

"Yes," he agreed tersely. "Thank God."

She couldn't answer that. She opened the door and walked ahead of him.

Bess wasn't there. Bobby looked up with a sly grin. "Bess has gone for a walk on the beach," he murmured. He cleared his throat. "I guess you two settled your differences...."

Elissa blushed to the roots of her hair. King laughed delightedly and slid his arm around her. "It wasn't anything serious," he said, chuckling. "I'm sorry if we embarrassed you."

Bobby shrugged. "Not me. But Bess is unusually sensitive, I guess." He put down his pen. "She and I used to be like that, but she's grown away from me. So many parties and teas and girls' nights out—I hardly see her when I'm at home."

"You might try spending more time there, now that you can afford to," King suggested pointedly.

"I might. I think I'll stroll out and join her."

"We'll make some coffee," King said, and he led Elissa toward the kitchen.

"She was hurt," Elissa said as she filled the coffeepot.

"I know." His voice was deep and curt, and he was staring out the window at Bess watching the waves.

She plugged in the pot and went to him, touching his chest lightly where the shirt was unbuttoned. "And so are you," she said gently. "I'm sorry. I feel as if I've failed you."

"How?" he asked, smiling.

"I couldn't give myself."

"The hell you couldn't." He chuckled wryly, then linked his arms around her waist and looked down at her. "*I* stopped us. You didn't. Not even when I mentioned pregnancy."

She lowered her eyes to his chest. "I'm not so afraid of it."

"Aren't you?" He studied her. No, she didn't seem to be. And he was shocked to learn that he wasn't, either. That intrigued him. Shouldn't he have been?

He turned to gaze out the window once more.

Five

___

Are you sure Bess doesn't want children?'' Elissa asked abruptly, disrupting his disturbing thoughts.

He turned back toward her. "She says not," he replied. Hands in his pockets, he leaned against the counter. "In the beginning, I think it was because she didn't want to be tied down. Her mother had seven children." He smiled sadly, remembering. "Bess was in the middle, but she did her share of looking after the little ones. She had a rough time of it, and so did the other kids, for that matter," he murmured, remembering how Bess's father drank and terrified the children. "Anyway, children don't necessarily guarantee a good marriage. I've seen happy marriages destroyed by them."

That sounded very private. "Have you?"

He frowned. "My mother often said that she and my father were happy enough until I came along and spoiled things," he said quietly.

"What a horrid thing to say to your own child," Elissa muttered, her face taut as she arranged cups and saucers and cream and sugar on a big silver tray.

"My mother was a devoted socialite," he said. "She didn't much care for children. If my stepfather hadn't insisted, Bobby probably would never have been born. Odd how things turn out. She was a vivacious, beautiful woman with a quick mind. And now she's a shell of her former self."

"Do you visit her very often?"

"As often as I can," he said. "She doesn't know me, of course."

She studied his hard face while the coffee finished perking, thinking how difficult his childhood must have been. She felt a burst of sympathy for the boy he had been.

"It wasn't that rough," he said after a minute, clearly reading her expression. "Besides, it was an incentive to show them all what I could do. Hasn't anyone ever told you that revenge has produced a hell of a lot of successful men?"

"I suppose so. Is that why you've never married? Because of your own childhood?" she persisted gently.

He sighed. "Oh, Elissa," he murmured, smiling. "You're one of a kind, honey."

"I just wondered," she said.

He watched her pour coffee into the elegant floral china cups, thinking how sweetly domestic she seemed at that moment. She could cook like an angel, she looked exquisite in anything she put on, she had a gentle and loving nature, and physically she made the top of his head fly off with the uninhibitedness of her response to him.

"If I ever married, I suppose it would be you," he said unexpectedly.

Her hand trembled, spilling coffee. She put the pot down with shaky fingers and reached for a dish towel to mop up the mess.

"That was unkind," she told him.

"I meant it, in fact," he said lazily, moving closer. "There's not much hope of marriage in my life, with things the way they are. But I think I could enjoy living with you. You're quiet and amusing, and I covet your body."

He was openly leering at it, in fact, and she burst out laughing. It was a joke, of course. After all the time she'd known him, occasionally it was still difficult to tell when he was joking.

"I covet yours, too, but I'm not that kind of girl," she reminded him primly.

"That doesn't stop you from looking out windows at nude men at night, I notice," he said, tongue in cheek.

She threw up her hands. "Well, if that's the attitude you're going to take, I'll find some other nude man to ogle!"

"What was that?" Bobby asked from the doorway, laughing. Behind him, Bess was glaring at them both.

Elissa flushed. "Now see what you've done? Your brother will think I'm a voyeur."

"Well, aren't you?" King grinned.

She handed him the tray. "I hope you drop it on your foot," she said sweetly.

"Vicious woman," he muttered. "Open the door, honey," he told Bess.

Bess flushed, and the two of them exchanged a look that made Elissa want to throw herself off a building. Fortunately, Bobby had gone ahead and didn't see it. Elissa wished *she* hadn't. King might want her body, but what she saw in his eyes when he looked at Bess was something she'd have died for. It was a sweeping kind of hunger, mingled with tenderness.

Bess curled up on the sofa to drink her coffee, pausing now and again to glance at Elissa, who knew that everything she and King had done probably showed in her lack of makeup and tangled hair.

"I hope we're not intruding by staying here tonight," Bess said quietly. "But the hotel was so crowded, and you're much closer to the airport than we were, way up in Ocho Rios."

"You're not intruding at all," King replied. He glanced at Elissa. "Elissa will need tonight to pack and get the cottage squared away, won't you, baby?"

"That's right," she said. It was hard to talk when he called her "baby." "And I'd better get to it if we're leaving in the morning. What time is it?" she added, rising.

"You'll need to be ready by eight," he said. He got lazily to his feet. "I'll walk you home," he said with a meaningful smile. "Don't wait up," he told the other two.

"I need an early night myself," Bess said coolly. "I expect I'll be out like a light in no time."

"I wish I could say the same," Bobby muttered over his paperwork. "I won't finish before dawn, at this rate. I guess you wouldn't care to help?" he asked Bess.

Her eyes widened. "Me? Heavens, I can't add one and one."

"Too bad," Bobby said. He seemed about to say something else, but he shrugged and bent his head again. "See you in the morning, Elissa."

"Sleep well," she told them, clinging to King's hand as he led her out into the darkness.

He lit a cigarette and smoked it during the short walk to her cottage, not saying a word. It was a warm, pleasant night, even with the misting rain around them.

At the back step of her cottage, he ground out the cigarette. "I'm sorry about this trip, but I couldn't think of another way to do it that didn't involve you."

"It's all right. I'm not doing so well with the new designs, anyway. I'll let them go for a week or two and touch base with some of my contacts back home."

"You still live with your parents, don't you?" he asked.

"Well, there's been no reason not to," she reminded him. "They'd be hurt if I wanted to live alone in Miami, and New York is pretty far away. We've been close all my life."

"I wouldn't know what that kind of closeness was," he admitted. "I like Bobby well enough, but we've never been really affectionate. I've never felt that way about any of my family."

"I'm sorry, because it's a special feeling."

"I suppose it is." He bent and brushed his lips carelessly over hers. "I'll go for a walk before I head back. Don't answer the phone for the next hour, in case Bess calls to see what's going on over here."

She tugged at his shirt sleeve as he turned. "I could make you some hot chocolate," she said shyly.

He lifted her hand to his mouth and kissed its warm palm. "I could take you to bed, too."

She looked up at him in the light from her kitchen. "King . . ."

His face went taut. "Elissa, I enjoy making love to you. I could make a banquet of your body. I even like you. But if I seduced you, what would we do?"

She blinked. "I don't understand."

He cupped her face in his hands. "Listen to me, little one. Sex is a loaded gun. Once you have it with someone, it involves you in ways you might not realize. I can't become involved with a virgin."

"After the first time, I wouldn't be a virgin," she reminded him.

He sighed angrily. "After the first time, you might wish you still were," he said bluntly. "You've been raised to think of sex as a sin outside marriage. How are you going to feel about yourself and me if I let that happen? Besides which," he added, "there's always the risk that you could get pregnant. And that's a complication neither of us is ready for."

She smiled wistfully, shaking her head.

"What does that mean?" he asked.

"I was just picturing you, your first time with a woman, going through all that with her," she said on a grin.

He cocked his head a little and smiled slowly. "My first time," he said in a loud whisper, "was so damned fast she hardly knew what was going on."

Her face slowly went scarlet, and he laughed. "Did you expect that the first time is always good for a man?" He grinned. "Men aren't born knowing how to make love. It takes experience to make bells ring and the earth move. After my first fumbling attempts, I had to work up the courage even to try again."

"I can't quite imagine that," she mused, smiling.

He nuzzled his forehead against hers, sighing. "Funny, I can tell you things I've never told anyone else," he murmured. "I must feel safe with you."

"I feel safe with you," she echoed. "That was why I latched on to you at the very beginning. You never tried to put the make on me."

"Until now," he corrected, lifting his head to search her eyes. "Are you sorry I didn't let things go on as they were?"

"No," she said almost at once. "Even though I can't imagine lying with any other man like that, I know I'd have let you do anything you wanted to," she admitted, "and I would have gloried in it. I don't even have enough pride to refuse you; it's too wonderful."

His eyes narrowed in pain, and his hands tightened on her oval face. "You shouldn't be quite that honest," he teased gently. "I'm only human. I might lose my head one night."

Her lips parted on a soft sigh. "I'll bet you're very good in bed," she whispered shyly.

"So I've been told," he said, laughing. His hands caressed her shoulders. "Look, we have to stop talking about sex," he murmured, "or we'll both be in trouble." He sighed. "What a mess. What a hell of a mess."

"It will all work out," she said. She stood on tiptoe to touch her lips to his eyelids. They closed tremulously, and she drew her mouth over them, amazed at the sudden stiffening of his body, the catch of his breath. She drew away, but his hands caught her waist and held her there.

"Don't stop," he breathed roughly. "I like it."

"Do you?" She repeated the soft little caresses, then instinctively smoothed kisses over his thick eyebrows, his lean cheeks and high cheekbones, down to his very sensuous mouth.

He was breathing rapidly, and she liked that. She remembered what he'd said to her that first time, driving her wild, and with her lips poised near his, she whispered, "Open your mouth."

It was like setting a match to dry wood. He seemed to go up in flames. His arms lifted her, crushing her against him, and his mouth invaded hers with a sensuous insistence. He was trembling, and his loss of control inspired both fear and wonder in her.

"Yes," she whispered when he backed her up against the door and fit his body to hers. "Yes!"

His rhythmic movements should have shocked her, but they were pure delight. She arched into them, her pride gone with her inhibitions, her arms curved around his neck, her mouth smiling under his as she gasped with pleasure.

She felt his hands moving on her body, gliding down to her hips, easing up the skirt of her dress. His urgent fingers felt cool on her hot skin, so welcome, so right. She moaned.

He lifted his head for an instant to breathe, his eyes frightening, his body shuddering. "Crazy child," he ground out, glaring at her. Then he moved against her, deliberately. "Feel that! Don't you know what you're asking for?"

"Heaven," she whispered, feeling deprived when he pulled away from her and turned his back.

"Heaven," he chided. He lifted his head, gulping in deep breaths, hating his loss of control and almost hating her for causing it. He'd never let a woman affect him so deeply. He fumbled for a cigarette. It was because she was a virgin, of course. She didn't know what she was doing. She was experimenting, and her innocence caused her to do things that a more experienced woman would know better than to try.

"Damn you!" he burst out, half laughing, half groaning.

She was still leaning against the door where he'd left her, breathless but smiling. He was as vulnerable to her as she was to him, she knew now. That was encouraging. Perhaps he did feel drawn to Bess, who was more or less using him to salve her tortured ego, but his emotional involvement with the other woman wasn't total. It couldn't be, or he wouldn't hunger so for Elissa. For perhaps the first time in her life she consciously felt a surge of pride in her own womanhood, in her ability to reach him. Her love life had been strictly fantasy until now, but King made her feel fiercely female and totally unafraid of him or anything he might do.

"Chicken," she purred.

He whirled, his black eyes narrowed in a face that was drawn with pain.

"What in hell are you trying to do?" he demanded.

"Lure you into bed with me," she said softly. "Come on. I dare you," she taunted with her newfound confidence.

He just stared at her. He had the cigarette in his lips now, but lighting it was another matter. He couldn't seem to hold the flame steady, and that brought a string of bitter curses to his lips.

She only smiled, coaxed the lighter from his lean fingers, flicked on the flame and held it to the cigarette.

"Proud of yourself?" he asked coldly. He smiled, but not happily.

"Proud of what I can do to you, yes," she confessed gently. "You seem so reserved at times, so unapproachable. It's nice to know you're human."

"You almost found out exactly how human," he muttered.

Her eyes searched his, and she sighed softly. "I tingle all over. That was so sweet."

"Not for me," he said through his teeth.

She watched his face, frowning a little. "I don't understand."

"I know." He took a deep draw from the cigarette and turned away, walking down the beach.

She followed, puzzled. "Can't you talk about it?"

He reached out, drawing her gently against his hips. His voice at her temple was slow and thick with discomfort. "I ache for you," he whispered. "Badly. Have you forgotten what we talked about, how after a certain point it's difficult to pull back?"

"I wasn't going to stop you," she reminded him.

"We couldn't very well make love on the beach in full view of my family!" he burst out. "Where's your mind tonight?"

"I don't know," she sighed. "I ache in places I never knew I had, I'm burning up with desire, and here you are, fully capable of putting out every fire I've got, and you're complaining that you're in pain."

He couldn't help it; he burst out laughing. "Oh, my God," he moaned.

She threw up her hands. "I offer you myself, no strings attached, and you walk off in a snit."

"Your parents would be ashamed of you," he pointed out.

"My parents don't expect me to be superhuman," she shot back. "God made bodies, you know, so I guess He expected that people would want to enjoy them occasionally."

"Although you'd rather do so with a ring on your finger," he prodded.

She shrugged. "Yes. But that doesn't cool me off any."

"Cool, the devil." He flung the cigarette away and lifted her suddenly, carrying her into the surf. "I'll cool you off."

He dumped her into the next wave. She spluttered and struggled to her feet, her dress plastered to her body, her hair in strings down her back.

"Wild animal!" she raged.

"Sexy baggage," he returned. "Want to hit me? Come on. Try it."

She took a swing at him. He sidestepped, and she went down again, and before she could get up he was in the water beside her, holding her down.

There was a look in his eyes that she'd never seen, and the sheer strength of his hands excited her. "You can't very well wear it like that, can you?" He laughed softly as he felt her bedraggled dress. "Let me help you out of it."

"You can't! Not here!" she gasped, looking around wildly.

"Yes I can," he shot back, and he began unfastening the soaking dress.

The surf crashed around them while he undressed her, and she reveled in the contrast between the cool water and her heated flesh, in the lazy contact of his hands, in the look on his dark face as he uncovered and savored every soft inch of her, his eyes lingering on her full breasts.

"God, what a beauty you are," he whispered. "I ought to strangle you for doing this to me."

"I'd like to point out that you're undressing me, not vice versa," she choked.

"You've seen me without my clothes," he said softly, searching her eyes.

"Yes." Her lips parted as she looked at him. "I wish we were alone. Totally alone."

"Stop tempting me," he whispered. After a minute, he reluctantly fastened the dress again and, with a heavy sigh, picked her up. His arms were strong and comforting against the night breezes. She snuggled closer, feeling unutterably cared for, and he bent to kiss her gently as he carried her up the beach. "You need to change and get some sleep. And in case you want to know, I'm leaving you at the door."

"Why?" she moaned against his lips.

"Sex makes babies," he whispered back. "I don't have anything to protect you."

She moaned again. "I don't care," she wailed.

"You would in the morning." He carried her to the door and set her slowly on her feet, taking a minute to run his hands over her and make her tremble with wanting.

"Sexy," he murmured. "Sexy and sweet, and I want to bury myself in you. Now you'd better get inside and try to sleep."

"Don't go," she whispered. "You're soaking wet, too."

"I can't very well walk home without my clothes." He chuckled. "Go to bed."

She shivered. "I can't."

"Why not?"

"My house key is in my pocketbook. Inside," she added with a faint flush. "Well, I forgot when I locked the door..."

He looked heavenward. "Women!" He searched until he found the spare key she hid under the hibiscus bush. "Here. I remembered, even if you didn't."

She looked up at him, her heart shaking her. He was so much man. So big and capable and strong, and just for once she liked being dependent, letting him take care of her. She thought about how it would be, having him beside her in the darkness, holding him through the night. Just holding him would be enough, she realized suddenly. What she felt was overpowering but not entirely physical. It was so tender, so sweet and new. If only he could feel it for her.

He unlocked the door and opened it, glancing down at her expression curiously. "What's wrong?" he asked, pressing the key into her palm.

"Nothing, really."

He reached in and switched on the light, then looked at her, drinking in the contours of her body now clearly visible through the dress plastered wetly to her skin. He shook his head. "You'll be the death of me one day. I'll have a heart attack trying to be noble."

"I won't take the blame," she said pertly.

"I won't take *you*," he whispered, bending to brush a chaste kiss on her forehead. "Now go to bed, siren. We've got an early flight."

"All right."

He handed her a shawl from the hat rack, watching her wrap herself in it. "Why do you want me all of a sudden?" he asked gently. "You've spent two years keeping me at arm's length. What's changed?"

"I never knew how devastating it could be," she said shyly.

"It shocks me a little, too," he said honestly. "You're not exactly my usual kind of woman."

"Maybe that's why you want me," she essayed.

He sighed. "I don't know. All I know is that for the past twenty-four hours, you're all I've thought about. But I can't afford to lose my head. Your conscience would torment you to death."

"But I don't want to lose you. You're my friend." Her eyes filled with unshed tears at the thought.

"Don't cry," he ground out. "I can't stand it."

She lifted her face. "Sorry. I was looking ahead. One of us will eventually marry, I guess," she added, thinking that it would probably be King. "And that will be the end of us, anyway."

He studied her, scowling. It hadn't occurred to him that he might ever have to lose her. But she was right: she would probably marry eventually, and her husband might not take kindly to their unusual friendship. There would be no more long walks along a Jamaican beach, no more phone calls at two in the morning just because he needed someone to talk to, no more laughing Elissa leaving him notes under rocks....

"I'll miss having you to talk to," she confessed softly.

He shifted restlessly. "I was thinking the same thing," he said quietly. "I'm alone except for you." Before she could reply, he turned and opened the door. "I'll see you in the morning."

He closed it and left her standing there.

Alone, in the harsh light of reality, she was astounded at her behavior. Letting fantasies take over, she had offered to... Her face flamed, and she caught her breath. She'd acted like a total wanton with King.

She got out of her wet things, put on a caftan and dried her hair, troubled by the direction her life was taking. If she truly became King's lover, would she be discarded when he tired of her? She loved him, but she knew he merely wanted her. She had to get her perspective back, and she couldn't do that around King. All in all, it was best that she was going home.

Unbidden, the memory of what King had said before leaving came back to her: "I'm alone except for you." What had he meant by the statement?

She was still puzzling over it when she went to bed.

Six

Riding to the airport was an ordeal. Although Elissa sat in the front seat with King, his eyes kept darting to the rearview mirror. He talked to Bobby, but it was Bess he was exchanging eloquent looks with.

The one thing it did accomplish was to make Elissa see clearly what a fool she'd been to daydream over his exquisite lovemaking. He'd only been toying with her; there hadn't been anything serious about it on his part. Probably he'd made love to dozens of women without feeling the need to commit himself. Men weren't like women, she told herself; they didn't need emotional involvement to find fulfillment. But it saddened her all the same. She'd just begun to realize how much she cared about him, how much a part of her life he'd become. She'd looked forward to coming to Jamaica, not because of the island itself but because of the man who lived next door. And she felt possessive about him.

That possessiveness had reared its ugly head the instant she saw Bess. It hadn't taken much effort to realize how appealing King's sister-in-law must be to him. She wasn't a shallow flirt just out for a good time. She was beautiful and vulnerable and unhappy, tied to a man she cared about who never paid her any attention. How terrible that must feel, and how much King must want to comfort and protect her. But how terrible, too, for King to be torn between his feelings for Bess and for Bobby and his sense of what was right. What a mess.

And what a pity, Elissa thought, that she herself couldn't be one of those superficial people who enjoyed life without really considering consequences. But she knew herself too well to think she could survive a casual affair with King. Her principles were too firmly embedded in her personality, and despite her abandon when she was with him, he was right that her conscience would kill her if she fell into his bed. Besides, she thought miserably, would he still feel the same about her once he'd been intimate with her? She didn't think she could stand to have him and then lose him.

And what about Bess? Did she really want King, or was she attracted to him because he was safely unattainable and no real threat to her marriage? Elissa sighed, staring at the passing sea-grape trees and tall casuarina pines that partially veiled the blinding white beach and the incredible blues and greens of the Caribbean. What a ridiculous question. Her eyes turned to King, adoring his profile. He was handsome and rich, and what he didn't know about women wasn't worth knowing. Who wouldn't want him for keeps? She looked away quickly and closed her eyes on a wave of pain. If he and Bess wound up together, they would undoubtedly marry and have children. How that thought hurt!

Time crawled while they got through the long line of customs and immigration before boarding the plane. Bess eased into the seat next to King's on the enormous jumbo jet, and Elissa, on his other side, couldn't help but notice the way Bess clutched his hand as the plane prepared for takeoff.

"Frightened?" King asked his sister-in-law in a tone so tender that it hurt Elissa.

"Not now," Bess whispered, her heart in her eyes.

Elissa looked away, unable to bear the tender smiles they were exchanging. Across the aisle, Bobby, once more buried in his paperwork, hadn't even noticed.

When they touched down in Miami, Elissa breathed a sigh of relief. Sitting next to King and Bess had been utter torment, but now she could escape. She could go home to her parents and try to forget all about this. She didn't ever want to see the two of them together again. If that meant selling her cottage, well... The thought was horrifying. She couldn't bear it if she never saw King again! Her eyes filled with hot tears, and she swallowed them down before he could see them. How had this happened? They'd been friends. She almost wished he'd never touched her. She could almost hate him for making her so aware of him, of her feelings for him.

They cleared customs and immigration again, and Elissa stood a little apart while King said goodbye to Bobby and Bess.

"We need to get going," he told them, "so we won't wait to wave you off. I'll be back to the ranch in a week or so. Check with Blake Donavan and make sure everything's all right. He's supposed to be looking out for me while my foreman's on vacation."

"Imagine Donavan having time to do that," Bobby said with a laugh. "The last I heard, he was up to his ears trying to hold on to his own place after his uncle died. All those greedy cousins of his, filing lawsuits..."

King chuckled. "Donavan won, didn't you hear? Hell of a businessman."

"And a dish," Bess said playfully, glancing surreptitiously at Bobby. "He's never married, either. I wonder why not. Do you suppose he's nursing some hopeless passion for someone?"

No one responded to Bess's musings, but Elissa saw King's face harden. Then he forced a smile as he shook Bobby's hand. "Take care of yourself and Bess."

"Sure, sure. Thought we might find some time to go horseback riding this weekend," he added with a grin at Bess, who looked amazed. "Bess and I might pack a picnic lunch."

"You on a picnic?" Bess murmured. "Do you go with or without your pocket calculator?"

"Don't be catty, you sweet little thing," Bobby said, chuckling. "See you, Elissa. King will have to bring you out sometime and show you the place."

"That would be nice," Elissa murmured politely.

Bess didn't say goodbye to either of them, except to force a smile and wave as she walked ahead of Bobby down the terminal.

King watched her, his heart in his eyes. Elissa couldn't bear that, so she picked up her carryall and began to walk toward the exit.

"Where the hell do you think you're going?" he demanded, falling into step beside her to reach for her bag with an impatient hand.

"Home," she replied. "There's no need for you to come with me. You're perfectly safe now. You can check into a hotel somewhere and—"

"I said I'd take you home," he reminded her, his tone cool and authoritative. "Sit over there while I arrange about a car."

She did, angrily, still wounded by having watched him with Bess. She had to get herself under control, she thought. It wouldn't do to let him see how deeply involved with him she'd become.

She gave a brief thought to her parents and how they were going to react to having her home so unexpectedly. At least she didn't have to worry about King's meeting them; he'd probably be glad to let her off at the gate of their modest house outside Miami and rush off.

But when King pulled up at her parents' beachfront house and surveyed the surrounding dunes and the waves of the Atlantic rolling lazily to shore behind it, he seemed in no hurry to leave. He gazed at the hibiscus lining the front walk, along with the graceful palms and a banana tree her mother had planted years before, took in the white front gate and the lounge furniture on the porch and remarked, "It reminds me of your cottage in Jamaica."

"They're similar. Well, thanks for the ride." She started to get out of the car, but he clasped her wrist, then her fingers.

His eyes were very dark, looking into hers. Puzzled. Faintly disturbed. "You've been quiet. Too quiet."

She shifted restlessly. She didn't want him asking questions or making assumptions. "My parents aren't expecting me," she muttered. "I'm trying to figure out what to tell them."

"Tell them a hurricane blew over your cottage," he suggested, tongue in cheek.

"What a cheerful man you are," she replied, staring at him. "Why don't you go into comedy for a living?"

"Stop fighting me," he murmured as she tugged against his firm but gentle hold. "You'll hurt my ego."

"It could stand a little deflation," she said crisply, glaring at him.

Comprehension took the playful expression from his face, leaving his eyes narrow and glittering. He dropped her hand. "She can't help it any more than I can," he said, his tone cold and cutting.

"So I noticed." She reached for the door handle. "Good thing for you both that your half brother is blind as a bat and keeps his nose stuck in his papers. Those quiet types are the ones who go for their guns without asking for explanations. You and Bess would look lousy on the front page of the tabloids, full of bullet holes."

"Would we?" he asked with surprising mildness. "You seem to find the idea satisfying."

She grabbed her carryall and slammed the door, about to add something cutting. But just as she opened her mouth, her mother, clad in a flapping red-splashed muumuu, came rushing through the gate like a barefooted, white-haired tornado.

"Darling!" she enthused, grabbing her daughter up in a fierce hug, her blue eyes dancing with glee. "Oh, what a delicious surprise! Your father will be overjoyed! He's just bought another crawly for his collection and wants to show it off to someone— Who are you?" she added, staring over Elissa's shoulder as King came around the car.

"Kingston Roper," he answered easily, studying the tall, thin woman. "You must be Elissa's mother."

"Yes, I am. I'm Tina Dean." Her mother withdrew a little, her blue eyes confused and a little curious. "Is something wrong?"

"King is my neighbor in Jamaica," Elissa said. "He was kind enough to offer me a lift from the airport. We flew over with his brother and sister-in-law." She could see that Tina Dean was quietly sizing him up, taking in his tailored suit, his hand-stitched shoes, his silk tie and expensive accessories. She could almost hear her mother's mind clicking, sorting through what Elissa had told her of her friendship with King and trying to put two and two together about what this obviously wealthy man was doing with her daughter.

"I have some iced tea in the kitchen," she remarked. "Would you like some, Mr. Roper?"

"King has to get back to Miami," Elissa said firmly, staring up at him. "Don't you?" she emphasized.

"Not at all," he replied with a maddening smile. "I'm in no hurry."

"Delightful," Mrs. Dean said with a grin. Her eyes twinkled. "How do you feel about reptiles, Mr. Roper?"

"Well, I used to have a pet horned toad," he began.

"Oh, Mother, no," Elissa moaned, putting her face in her hands.

King gave her a curious glance before Mrs. Dean took his hand and led him into the house.

Elias Dean was in his study, where he kept his collection of exotic lizards. He looked up, his thick silver hair slightly receding from his broad forehead, his eyes covered by thick spectacles with wire rims. At the sight of his daughter he beamed and greeted her warmly. Then he turned his attention to their new visitor.

"Well, hello, who's this?" he asked pleasantly, rising from a terrarium with a big frilled green lizard in one hand.

King offered a hand, apparently unruffled by the "crawlies." "Kingston Roper." He grinned. "You must be Elissa's father."

"That I am. Do you like lizards, Mr. Roper? This is my hobby." He sighed, looking around him contentedly at terrarium after terrarium. "I can't ever seem to get enough, you know. It's up to ten curly-tails now, several spring lizards, newts, salamanders... But this is my pride and joy." He reached for a door and opened it. Inside was an enormous pool with potted tropical plants all around it. On a rock in the pool under a fluorescent lamp was Ludwig, a four-foot iguana who looked like a dinosaur. He stared at them with total boredom and closed his eyes.

"Iguana?" King asked, clearly interested.

"Yes. Isn't he beautiful?" her father asked. "He was only a baby when I got him. I had to force-feed him the first week with a big syringe, until he took fruits and vegetables on his own. I like frogs, too. I want one of those huge African frogs—they weigh ten pounds. She doesn't like frogs," he added with a miserable glance at Tina.

Tina laughed. "You're just lucky I don't mind lizards, Elias. Although I did draw the line at that ball python you were ogling. Snakes disturb me." She shuddered. "Lizards are bad enough."

"I have to have a hobby, my dear," he reminded her. "It could be worse. Do you remember that witch doctor we met down the Amazon, the one who collected heads?"

"I withdraw every objection," Tina promised, hand over her heart. "Would you like tea, darling? I'm going to pour some for Elissa and her... and Mr. Roper."

"I'll be out directly," Elias promised. "I have to feed poor old Ludwig."

"Poor old Ludwig," Tina chuckled as they made their way back down the hall to the kitchen, where sliding doors opened onto a deck facing the ocean. "He takes him walking down the beach on a leash. It's a good thing we have such a loyal congregation." She shook her head.

"Father is eccentric," Elissa said quietly, glancing worriedly at King.

He cocked an eyebrow. "My father collected rocks," he remarked. "And I had a great-uncle who could forecast the weather with jars of bear grease. Compared to that, keeping lizards seems pretty sane."

Elissa leaned back in her chair. "Go ahead, Mother, tell him what you do in your spare time," she dared, watching Tina pour amber tea into tall glasses of ice.

King frowned slightly and turned to Tina. "What do you do in your spare time?"

Tina set the glasses on the small kitchen table. "Well, I'm a special deputy for the sheriff's department."

"Now, that sounds interesting," King said, and he seemed to mean it.

"It's very interesting," she agreed. She got her own tea and sat down. "I have so much experience as a missionary, you see, it gives me a little insight into people. Some of the folks we arrest are women, and I seem to deal with them better than the men do." She smiled wistfully. "I've been on drug busts and in shoot-outs and stakeouts, and once I jumped a fence and wrestled down a young pusher and held him for the deputies. Yes, it's exciting and very rewarding. I often look up the people later and try to get to know them." Her eyes softened. "I've managed to get several of them to come to services on Sunday. And we baptized one just last week," she added, her voice a little husky. "I suppose this sounds pretty saccharine to a worldly man like you."

"But I'm not," King said, surprising even Elissa. "I was raised a Baptist in Jack's Corner, a small town outside Oklahoma City, near my ranch. My father was Apache, but he bowed to some white customs. He found church fulfilling for a time."

Elissa was stunned at how easily King related to her mother. He'd even volunteered information about his heritage, which he was usually so prickly about.

"Apache," Tina said, studying him more closely with totally innocent curiosity. "Yes, your eyes are very dark, and you have high cheekbones...."

"Mother," Elissa groaned, "he's not an exhibit."

King chuckled. "Elissa is remembering that I can get touchy about my ancestry," he remarked with a smile in Elissa's direction. "I don't mind honest curiosity. I don't suppose you see many Indians in this part of the country."

Tina grinned. "I guess I don't look it," she told him, "but I'm part Seminole, on my mother's side."

King's eyebrows rose. "You never told me," he murmured to Elissa.

She shrugged. "You never asked about my ancestry."

He frowned. That was true. They often shared their thoughts and feelings and dreams, and he'd even told her about his family, but he'd never bothered to ask about hers. He felt oddly guilty about that now and inordinately curious to know more about this little spitfire.

"My grandfather had a Seminole name, which he changed," Tina continued, looking at King. "Is Roper your father's real name?"

King smiled and told her the Apache word for Man Who Throws Rope. "That's why he changed it to Roper," he added.

"Do you like to fish, Mr. Roper?" Elissa's father asked, coming into the kitchen.

"If you mean deep-sea fishing, no," King replied. "But if you mean dipping a worm on a hook into a creek, yes."

Mr. Dean grinned. "My sentiments exactly. There's a nice little swamp about two hour's drive from here, where you can get some of the biggest bream and crappie you ever saw."

"We have a spare room," Tina Dean added, smiling at him. "It's quiet here; we're off the main drag. I see that Elissa looks horrified, but we won't let the lizards eat you, and if you're as tired as you look, the change might do you good, Mr. Roper."

Elissa went red. She'd forgotten how outspoken her mother was. She did look horrified. She felt horrified. Don't do this to me, she wailed silently. He's in love with another woman, and I want to get away from him.

King turned toward Elissa and saw that look on her face. "If you don't want me to stay, I won't," he said gently.

The soft tone made her toes curl. What could she say? "I don't mind," she murmured.

"I must look tired if it shows that much," he said, winking at Mrs. Dean. "Yes, I'll stay, thank you."

"Wonderful!" Mr. Dean chuckled. "We'll find some lazy projects to keep you relaxed."

"I'll fatten you up," Mrs. Dean seconded, giving him a critical glance. "You look undernourished."

Elissa could have laughed. He might look trim, but he was very muscular under his shirt. She flushed, wondering what her parents would say if she confessed that she'd watched

him swim in the nude from her cottage window. She forced
a smile and finished her iced tea while her mother asked
about his work. He replied that he was in oil and gas. It
didn't dawn on Elissa until much later how her mother had
interpreted that remark.

"To think, a handsome man like that working in a garage," Mrs. Dean sighed as she made supper.

"What?" Elissa asked sharply.

"Well, he's in oil and gas," she explained patiently, "and
despite the nice-looking suit he's wearing, which he might
have borrowed, I think his watch and ring are only copies of
expensive ones. He's trying to impress us, darling, to show
us that he'd be a good catch for you. I'm very flattered. I
like him. So does your father. And there's nothing wrong
with working in a garage. His parents probably own it, you
know, and that's probably their home in Jamaica. They
must just let him use it."

Boy, had her mother gotten it wrong. But Elissa bit her
tongue. This was better. They didn't need to know how rich
King really was; it might inhibit them. She liked their response to him, and his to them. She couldn't bear to spoil
it. She'd tell them later, after King was gone.

Her eyes closed. Despite her trepidations, it was marvelous to have him in her home, to savor being with him away
from Bess's influence. She was in heaven. Even if he only
stayed overnight, she'd love the house forever afterward,
because she'd see him in every nook and cranny of it. And
if he married Bess, well, her dreams wouldn't harm the two
of them very much.

Seven

After supper, King and Elissa went for a stroll along the beach. It was very much like Jamaica at night, the white-caps rolling onto the beach with a foamy whisper.

"You don't mind that I'm here, do you?" he asked casually.

"No." She had changed into shorts and a long-sleeved shirt, and she was enjoying the feeling of the cool white sand on her bare feet. She tossed back her long hair and sighed, drinking in the peacefulness of the setting.

He was still wearing his slacks, but he'd unbuttoned his shirt halfway down and was wearing thongs instead of shoes. He looked very casual, not at all the elegant millionaire he really was.

"I didn't know you'd been raised a Baptist," she commented, turning her eyes seaward.

He glanced at her. "And I didn't know that you had Seminole blood."

She smiled. "I've got a little Irish, too, and a trace of German."

"I've got some Irish myself." He stopped her, gesturing toward a hermit crab diving into a hole in a small sandy bank. "I had one of those for a pet once. They're cute."

"With those claws?" she groaned.

"Claw, woman," he chided. "Well, one big one and one much smaller one. They don't pinch that hard."

"You wouldn't feel it with hands the size of yours, I guess."

He slid his hands into his pockets, stretching the expensive fabric of his slacks against the powerful muscles of his legs as he walked. "I like it here," he said lazily. "I like your parents, too. I can see now why you're such an independent little cuss. They're very open and honest."

She laughed softly, enjoying his company and the cool breeze and the solitude. "You'd really think so if you'd heard what my mother said about you."

He stopped, looking down at her. "What did she say?" he asked with interest.

"She says that you're very handsome to work in a garage, which your parents must own, and that that's their villa in Jamaica. They just let you use it. Your watch and ring are copies of the real thing, to impress them. Oh, and you probably borrowed that expensive suit you're wearing."

His eyebrows shot up, and he began to laugh, but not in a sarcastic or mocking way. It sounded like pure delight. "They think I'm a grease monkey?"

"You told them you were in gas and oil," she reminded him. "My parents don't know any oil magnates but they know a lot of mechanics."

"Well, I'll be damned," he mused. "I think I like that. Yes, I think I do. I haven't been treated like a normal human being in my adult life. At least not since I hit it big."

"You have so," she retorted. "Do I treat you like a big fish?"

He pursed his firm lips, then smiled at her, his white teeth gleaming in the pale light of the half moon. "Not really," he admitted. "That was one of the things I liked best about you. After I realized that you weren't chasing after me because I was rich," he added.

The cynicism in his voice touched her. "Did you really think that's why I kept hounding you?" She laughed. "How surprising."

"Women had chased me for years," he replied. "Once or twice I let myself be caught, but mostly I didn't give a damn for that kind of woman. It didn't take me long to learn that you weren't the least bit interested in my bank account. Then," he added with a wicked glance as he started walking again, "I decided it was my body you wanted."

"How conceited," she remarked airily.

"If you remember, I made one very subtle pass at you, right at the beginning," he said. "And you backed away with a look in your eyes I'll never forget. I didn't understand why you shied away from me. I thought you'd had some bad experience and were afraid of men. That made me even more protective, and I gave up any ideas of seducing you."

"Until a few days ago," she muttered.

His head jerked toward her. "Don't put all the blame on me, honey. You were giving as good as you got in my bed that night."

She was glad the darkness hid her blush. She stiffened a little as she shuffled along the beach beside him, oblivious now to the clamoring surf. Her legs were getting cold, but she didn't want to suggest that they go inside. Every second she could spend alone with him was a delight, even if it had to be spent in the middle of an argument.

"Thank you for that sterling assessment of my morals," she said lightly, forcing back a surge of fury. "I suppose that makes me what men call an easy—King!"

He jerked her around none too gently and shook her by both arms. "No, it doesn't make you easy," he said, his voice cold and curt. "Stop trying to make yourself sound cheap."

"Isn't that what you're trying to do?" she asked, hating the slight wobble in her voice.

His lean fingers tightened on her arms, exciting and strong through the flimsy sleeves of her oversize shirt. "I don't know what I'm trying to do," he said surprisingly. His hands relaxed, became caressing. He breathed slowly, deliberately, and drew her into his arms. He wrapped her against his taut body, enveloping her in his spicy cologne and his warmth, and laid his cheek on her dark hair.

It was, she thought suddenly, as if he needed comforting. And perhaps he did. He didn't say a lot about his feelings for Bess, but she was sure that he was confused and wounded by what was happening. He was willing to sacrifice his own happiness to keep from hurting Bess and Bobby, so he'd subdue what he felt for Bess or ignore it if he could. But with the women tempting him and, as he'd said, with his being only human, perhaps he did need comforting. And at the moment, Elissa was his anchor, his safety net, his life jacket. She didn't mind; it was enough to do what she could to help him through a difficult time. Love made you vulnerable. She knew, loving him as she did.

She slid her arms around his hard waist and pressed her cheek over his heart, enjoying the heavy, measured beat of it in the darkness. "We all want things that we can't have, from time to time," she began softly. "Like me, living a fantasy. I'd give so much to be like those women in the nighttime soap operas who have their fun and never have to suffer for it. But I'm too much of a coward to try it. I'd always worry about consequences and about hurting other people." She closed her eyes, breathing him in. "I always felt so free with you. I could tease, and you never took me seriously. I could try my wings, I could fly, without any danger of falling."

"Until one night you flew too close to the flame and singed your pretty wings," he murmured dryly. "Were you shocked?"

"Oh, yes," she confessed. "I didn't expect it, you see. And I didn't realize how vulnerable I might be."

"I did," he replied. His arms tightened. "We were both holding back for different reasons, bottling up our passions. Inevitably, it was going to get away from us one day. It just happened to be with each other. And I'm damned glad about that," he added curtly. "Another man might have taken advantage of it and seduced you for real."

She colored softly. "I can't imagine letting any other man do those things to me," she said honestly.

He actually shuddered. "Don't say things like that. I'm more vulnerable than you realize."

"Because she's gone."

He paused for an instant, and when his voice finally came, it was cold and measured. "Yes. Because she's gone. I did warn you that anything I did to you would be out of desire for her. Didn't you hear me?"

"I was too busy kissing you." She laughed gently.

He laughed, too, despite himself. "Imp," he muttered, tightening his arms and then loosening them to step away from her and look down into her quiet eyes. "You seemed to like kissing me."

She tossed back her head, living the dream all over again. "You have a nice mouth. Very slow, very experienced."

"Yours isn't bad, either," he murmured, dropping his eyes to it. He touched her cheek and traced her lips with his thumbs. "I'm sorry we're so close to the house. We could strip and go swimming."

"My father would let Ludwig eat you," she said with a laugh.

He sighed. "It was just a thought. I'd give a lot to see you out of your clothes, pretty thing."

That was embarrassing and a little exciting, all at once. "Well, you haven't missed much," she said.

"Not from the waist up, anyway," he agreed too readily, and laughed at her shocked little gasp. "God, you're sweet to tease. I'd forgotten that women could be shocked. Women in my set tend to be pretty blasé about sex."

"Probably because there isn't a lot they don't know about it." She tried to step back, but he caught her long hair and held her there in front of him.

"You're nervous of me," he murmured. "Why should you be? You could always scream for help."

"Yes, I know." She tugged at his hand. "I don't want to stand in for Bess, King."

"You told me that in the beginning. I haven't forgotten." He hesitated for a minute before he reluctantly let her go. "You sound positive enough about it."

His voice gave nothing away, but she thought he sounded a bit irritated. She tossed her hair and laughed up at him. "How would you feel if I kissed you and pretended you were some sexy man I wanted?"

His blood surged. "I'd break your sweet neck," he said without a second's hesitation.

She laughed even louder. "You see? Tit for tat, big man."

He made a swipe at her behind, and she barely sidestepped in time.

"If you hit me," she threatened, "I'll tell my daddy."

"Go ahead," he challenged. "I dare you."

"You ought to be shaking in your shoes," she replied. "He's got friends in high places."

He got her meaning and grinned, all his bad temper gone. "You know, I laugh more with you than I've ever laughed in my life," he remarked as they wandered back down the beach toward the brightly lit cottage.

"I don't think you even knew how to laugh at the beginning," she recalled. "You were a little frightening. All business and cold as ice."

"Cold on the outside," he said softly. "Never on the inside."

That was a blatant insinuation, and she ignored it. "Are you and Dad going fishing tomorrow?"

"Yes, we are." He glanced her way. "Are you coming with us?"

"I'd like to, but I've got to get in touch with Angel Mahoney and tell her I'm going to need another week on those new designs. Angel is vice-president of the Seawear collection, and she bought my designs for the chain of boutiques Seawear owns. I thought they were too strange for anyone," she confessed, "but Angel thought they were deliciously outrageous and very salable. And she was right. I'm making all kinds of money these days."

"It doesn't show," he said abruptly with a speaking glance at what she was wearing.

She lifted a haughty eyebrow. "I wouldn't waste my exquisite wardrobe on a mere friend," she informed him.

His dark eyes narrowed. "Is that all I am?"

"It's all I'm going to let you be," she said gently, looking away from him. "Would you like—"

"Why?" He was behind her in the shadow of the house, his hands around her waist pulling her back against his tautly muscled body.

"You know why," she ground out. The warmth of those hands was driving her wild.

"I can't have Bess," he whispered in her ear, drawing her even closer, "but I can have you. You can have me."

She trembled and closed her eyes as the tempting pictures rambled shamelessly in her mind. She gritted her teeth, because there was only one possible answer to the blatant seduction in his voice. "No."

"Tell me you aren't tempted, Elissa," he dared.

She pulled away from him, taking a few seconds to get her composure back. "How about some coffee?"

He hesitated at the back door, then sighed and gave in. He didn't understand himself lately. Elissa was suddenly in his blood, and he wanted her out. He hoped he wouldn't one day lose control with her. The thought frightened him a little. Yet he seemed to totally forget Bess when he touched Elissa. That was somehow frightening, too.

He followed her inside, his face thoughtful, to find her parents waiting to join them around the coffeepot. He smiled at them, relieved to find something to keep his mind occupied. It was having a field day with memories of Elissa, her dress disheveled and pushed down to her waist.

The next morning, King and Elissa's father set off before daylight. By the time Elissa and her mother were up, the men were long gone. Tina fixed a small breakfast for them and then set about her housework, while Elissa went down to the beach for a swim. Afterward, she set to work on her designs with a fierce determination to work off her frustrations on paper.

It worked, too; she came up with some totally new looks, very innovative and sexy and cool. She took a break for lunch and some lazy conversation with her mother, and then went back down to the beach, a flowered patio skirt over her one-piece black bathing suit, and stretched out on her towel to scribble some more.

The sun kept going in and out of the clouds. She closed her eyes with a sigh as it began to cool down, and she was almost asleep when a shadow fell over her.

She opened her eyes to King's dark face, his eyes narrow and speculative where the skirt had fallen away from her long, tanned legs. Her bodice had slipped because of the shoulder straps, almost baring one breast.

"Sexy as hell," he murmured, and there was irritation in his voice. "You look like a beached mermaid, and you'd better thank your lucky stars your parents are within earshot."

"Oh, promises, promises," she laughed drowsily, only half taking him seriously. She stretched, and his jaw tightened.

He unbuttoned his shirt, watching her the whole time, seeing how her attention suddenly became riveted on the hair-covered muscles he was revealing. When he stripped it off, her eyes widened on his torso, and he felt a surge of desire so strong that it almost knocked him to his knees. She liked looking at him. She was too inexperienced to hide her own longing, and the sight of it made him all to vulnerable to his own hungers.

"I thought I might go for a swim," he said huskily as his hand went to his belt.

Her lips parted. "You...can't," she began, thinking of her parents.

"I'm wearing trunks," he said. He unhitched the belt and slowly moved the zipper down. She was breathing quickly by the time he finally peeled the jeans down his long legs and discarded them, along with his sneakers.

"Why did you do that?" she asked in a strange, high-pitched tone when he turned to her.

"I like the way you look at me when I'm undressing," he said quietly, meeting her hesitant gaze. There was no mockery in his eyes, no teasing. He moved closer, looking down at her for a long instant before he caught one of her hands in his and put it against his chest. The hard muscles surged against it as he breathed, feeling the soft, silent searching of her cool fingers against his heated skin.

"My...my father?" she whispered, glancing down the beach.

"He's cleaning fish," he replied, searching her eyes. "Your mother is cooking."

"Oh."

He eased down alongside her, deftly unbuttoning her skirt. He pushed it aside, baring the smooth, exquisite lines of her body in the bathing suit. His hand went to the shoulder strap that was already almost off. He traced it down the fastening under her arm and, holding her shocked eyes, unhooked it.

"You mustn't, King," she said shakily. She caught his wrist, but it didn't even slow him down. He stared at her bodice, peeling it aside with steady, strong fingers, his thumb blatantly caressing her swelling breast and making her jerk with a sudden spasm of pleasure.

"Go ahead," he murmured curtly, bending his head. "Lie to me. Tell me you don't want this."

"What about . . . Bess?" she groaned, pushing at him.

He said something harsh and explicit that she only half heard, and then his head was against her body, his mouth taking her breast inside the warm darkness, teasing it with his tongue.

Her whimpers excited him. She didn't know how to hold back, and that was delicious. He slid his hands under her, smoothing her soft skin, lifting her closer to his ardent mouth.

She was trembling now, too far gone to protest anything he did to her. He moved one hand up her side to explore the exquisite softness of her breast while his mouth gently teased it. He lifted his head just enough to look, to watch his subtle tracing shatter her composure and bring a mist of tears to her blue eyes.

"Don't cry," he whispered, bending to touch his mouth to her eyelids and taste the salty moisture there.

"I hate you," she whimpered huskily.

He smiled indulgently. "No, you don't. You hate being vulnerable. So do I. But we enjoy each other too much to deny ourselves this pleasure. And it is pleasure, isn't it, Elissa?'' he whispered over her mouth. "Such wild, sweet pleasure.''

"But—''

He covered the word with his lips, brushing her mouth open with lazy, expert movements that made her body burn. She tried to protest, but he kept at it, slowing his movements, deepening them, tormenting her with little shivers of sensation that made her wild. He'd never kissed her like this before. It was as intimate as lovemaking. More intimate. She moaned, the sound as intimate as the kiss, as revealing as her shudders.

His free hand came up to her chin, cupping it, holding it firm. Above her, his body blocked out the sun, and his face was a stranger's, hard and faintly flushed, his eyes almost frightening.

"Yes,'' he whispered gruffly, continuing the subtle torment of her mouth, watching it open, feeling its aching sensuality. "Yes, you're ready for me, now, aren't you? Soft and submissive... oh, baby...''

His tongue penetrated her mouth in one slow, sharp thrust, his lips crushing down on hers.

She cried out, her trembling hands clutching his hair, her nails digging into his nape. She arched, shuddering, her body in sweet anguish as he felt her need and answered it, his hand swallowing her breast, softly cradling it. Her tongue tangled with his; her breathing seemed to stop. It was the most incredible sensation she'd ever felt in her life. Like flying into fire. Burning up. She was trembling all over and she couldn't stop, totally vulnerable and powerless to hide it from him.

She began to cry, tears rolling down to their feverishly joined mouths, sobs tearing from her throat, and still she clung, arching her body toward his hand.

"Elissa,'' he whispered in a tone he'd never used—achingly tender, almost loving.

He moved completely onto her shaking body, his weight exquisitely satisfying, his mouth tender now, his hands... He was doing something to her bodice, and then she felt his chest against her bare breasts, the hair on it tickling, the warm muscles gently spreading her swollen softness against them.

"Hold on tight," he whispered at her lips. "Hold me."

She couldn't stop crying. She buried her lips in his hot throat, shuddering under his weight, devastated by the feel of his body in such intimacy. He was aroused, and she felt that, too, and moaned.

"Sweet," he whispered at her ear, his fingers biting into her back. "Sweet, sweet Elissa!"

She bit his shoulder, a helpless reaction that she didn't even understand, and made a sound in her throat that curled his toes.

"Shh," he murmured. His fingers came to her cheek and soothed it, smoothing back her damp hair. His hand slid down to her waist and caressed it gently, while he whispered to her, tender little encouragements to relax, to lie still, to be quiet.

By the time she stopped shaking and could feel his taut body relaxing and losing its frightening hardness, her face was drenched in tears.

He rolled beside her then, still holding her, and onto his back. He pillowed her head on his shoulder, his arms betraying a fine tremor, while he stared blankly up at the sky, where sea gulls dived and called to each other against the gray clouds.

"I have to leave," he said after a minute, his voice harsh. "We can't go on like this any longer."

She knew that instinctively. He'd gone almost too far to stop, and so had she. She wasn't thinking anymore. Her body had a will of its own, too strong to fight. She closed her eyes and felt that she'd die if she couldn't have him just once.

"I know," she whispered. She sat up, her breasts swollen and slightly red from the pressure of his lips.

"Oh, baby," he breathed, looking as she covered them, his eyes blazing. "I could look at you forever."

"Don't." She closed her eyes, and he sat up, too, fastening the straps for her with hands that were a little unsteady.

"I don't know what's wrong with me lately," he confessed, forcing her to look at him. "I want you to the point of madness. You, Elissa. Not Bess." He looked down at her shoulders, delighting in their creamy perfection. "I don't understand why I feel this way, but if I don't have you, I think I'll die."

She understood that, because she felt the same way. "I want you just as much," she said quietly. "But afterward, I'll hate you," she added, looking up at him. "All those years of conditioning don't just vanish. I'll hate you, and myself, and I don't know how I'll live with it. But," she confessed shyly, looking at his chest, "I don't know how I'll live without it."

He got to his feet, pulling her up with him. His face was serious now, intent. "Come back to Oklahoma with me."

She moved restlessly, frightened of what they were discussing.

"Come with me," he repeated gently. He tilted her eyes up to his. "I promise I won't make you pregnant. I can't stop what's going to happen, but I'll make sure you're protected."

"No, I . . . I'll do that," she faltered. She looked toward the sea. "But how will we explain to my parents that I'm going back with you?"

He sighed wearily and touched her hair. "If it's any consolation, it bothers me, too." His fingers trailed down her cheek to her mouth, and he stared at it until her lips parted. "We'll tell them we may be getting engaged, and you're to stay with my family."

She looked up at him with stunned delight in her eyes, and the sight of it made him suddenly possessive. He jerked her against him.

"The hell with it—let's get married," he said suddenly. "I can't have Bess, and I've got to have you. Let's do it by the book."

She almost screamed "Yes!" at him, but she held back, sobered by the certainty that Bess would surely find some way to get to him eventually. It wouldn't do for Elissa to marry him and create even more problems. No matter how much it hurt, she was going to have to sink her pride and principles and give him the physical ease they both ached for. She loved him. If she had nothing else, she could have this. She could belong to him for a few ecstatic days, and then she would have to pay the piper. Somehow she'd survive the future. She and her memories of him.

"I won't marry you," she whispered gently. "But I'll go with you."

He frowned. "I don't mind—"

She put her fingers against his mouth. "You would, someday. Marriage should be a total commitment, a sacred thing, not just a legalization of desire. I hate what I feel for you, I hate what I'm going to do, but I think we'd regret marriage a lot more."

"It would ease your conscience afterward," he said tersely.

"And destroy yours," she countered. "Bess may...may be free someday. How would you feel if you were tied to me by then?"

His grimace gave her the answer. "It isn't fair, asking this of you."

"Life isn't fair sometimes," she said with a sigh, fighting tears. She looked up at him with the anguish of love in every line of her face. "Oh, King," she whispered softly, "I want you, too."

His hands tightened on her arms. "Come to see the ranch," he said, feeling guilty but unable to stop himself. "Just that. Maybe we can fight it."

That gave her a little hope. It would make it easier to explain to her parents if she wasn't definite about things. She smiled. "Okay."

He loved the way she smiled. Her eyes brightened, her face relaxed, she looked...beautiful. She *was* beautiful, inside and out. His body made an emphatic statement about its feelings for her, and he laughed in spite of himself.

"I'd better get dressed," he murmured dryly, turning away. He hadn't even been in the water, but he was drenched with sweat anyway.

She found her patio skirt and put it on, watching him pull on his jeans. It didn't embarrass her anymore when she knew he wanted her. It was so natural, as if she were already an extension of him, a physical part of him. She loved him to distraction.

He glanced at her, frowning at that rapt expression. She didn't seem to be afraid of him or nervous about giving herself to him. Why? Did she care for him? That made him tingle, and he turned to scoop up his shirt with a feeling he didn't understand. When he was dressed again, he took her hand, clasping it close in his without a single twinge about Bess.

"If it happens," he said without looking at her, "I'll make sure you never want to forget what we do together."

"I never would, whatever happened," she said solemnly.

He drew in a steadying breath and linked his fingers with hers. She made him feel ten feet tall. He couldn't understand this compulsion to make love to her; it wasn't only sex, but he couldn't puzzle out what else it was. He glanced down at her slender body, already picturing the very fluid way it was going to become part of him. He felt a flush of warmth from head to toe, and it got worse when he happened to drop his gaze to her flat stomach and involuntarily wondered what she'd look like with a baby in there.

His fingers clasped hers until they hurt, and she caught at them with curious laughter.

"What is it?" she asked breathlessly, wondering if he was thinking about Bess.

He searched her eyes. "Elissa . . . do you like children?" he asked slowly.

Inexplicably, she felt deliriously happy. He'd never asked a question like that. It gave her a little hope. She smiled, turning back toward the house. "Yes, of course. I'd like at least two someday. Why?"

He didn't answer her. His eyes were dark and troubled the rest of the way home. Bess said she didn't want children. And he was shocked to discover that he did. But he wanted them with Elissa.

He was totally withdrawn while he waited for the women to get supper together, electing to watch television with Mr. Dean. A telephone call he made a little later gave Tina the chance to ask Elissa what was wrong.

"He's asked me to his ranch," Elissa said with a smile. "I think he's worried about telling you and Dad."

Tina searched her daughter's face. "You're very much in love with him, aren't you, darling?"

Elissa sighed. "Yes. But he . . . I'm not sure he feels that way about me."

"He wants you." Tina smiled, but her eyes were solemn. "Be sure, honey. It's all too easy for a man to be physically infatuated, with no lasting emotion to hold him to a woman. I like your young man very much, but then, he's no threat to me."

Elissa put her head in her hands and leaned over her coffee cup, feeling lost and miserable. "I don't know what to do," she confessed. "I don't know if I can live without him now."

"My poor darling," Tina said quietly. She leaned over and kissed her daughter's forehead. "You have to find your own way, you know. I love you, and nothing you do will ever change that. I know your father and I must seem very old-fashioned to you, but we believe in what we do, and the way we live has to reflect that. Earthly pleasures are fleeting. Love is immortal, and it goes beyond satisfying some fleeting physical hunger. In other words, sweetheart," she explained with a grin, "sex won't make up for the lack of love, no matter how good it is."

"You hussy, talking like that," Elissa teased.

"That's me," Tina agreed. Her eyes twinkled. "You don't realize how much the world has changed in recent years. When I was in high school, girls could get expelled for wearing a skirt an inch above the knee. That was considered vulgar." She pursed her lips with a smile. "Life is so violent these days that I sometimes wish we were back in the Amazon," she muttered. "I felt safe there."

"I can help you out," Elissa said. "I'll bring Warchief over here to live with us and he can make you feel you're back in the jungle."

Tina, who'd heard volumes about the big parrot, frowned. "We have neighbors with sensitive ears."

"Our nearest neighbor is a mile down the beach," Elissa pointed out.

"That's what I mean. Sound carries. Besides," she groaned, "parrots fly. I have enough trouble with little bitty mosquitoes; imagine something that has wings and bites and weighs a pound."

Elissa had never thought of him as a giant green mosquito. She laughed. She'd have to remember to tell King. King. Her gaze softened. What was she going to do?

Tina patted her hand. "Life generally goes on," she reminded her daughter. "And God loves us. Even when we're naughty little girls and boys."

That was a comforting thought. Elissa got up and began to set the table.

Eight

Elissa's first sight of the Oklahoma plains drew a helpless sigh from her. Oklahoma City, where King had claimed his big gray Lincoln at the airport parking lot, was beautiful and intriguing for its rising oil derricks within the huge city itself. But the rolling plains, sweeping toward the horizon as far as the eye could see, brought tears to her eyes.

"I've never, ever seen anything like it," she breathed, her expression mirroring total delight.

King swerved the car as he darted a glance at her, fascinated. "I thought you'd hate it," he replied. "You live on the coast."

She wasn't even listening. "The Plains Indians—did they come down this far? The Sioux and Cheyenne?"

"Well, honey, Oklahoma was where they sent the Five Civilized Tribes back during the Trail of Tears, during the late 1830s and 1840s. Some of them fought for the Confederacy during the Civil War—a few were slaveholders, you see—and because of that, the government forced them to sell their western lands at a sacrifice. We have Chickasaws, Choctaws, Cherokees, Creek—and Seminole," he added after a pause.

Her face brightened. "No wonder it seems like home. Don't they say something about an ancestral memory? Perhaps some of my ancestors came here."

"The Seminoles were fierce warriors," he agreed easily. "They fought the government to a standstill."

"The Apache were pretty fierce, too, I hear," she murmured. She smiled at him and then turned her attention back to the undulating hills. "How beautiful. There's so much space, King."

"That's what I like about it. No crowding yet. Plenty of room. Oil and gas and cattle."

"The oil industry has been hard hit, though."

"Bobby and I had to diversify," he agreed. "But good business management will spare us too much grief. There it is." He indicated a dirt road leading to a grove of trees and a sprawling white frame house with huge porches. There were outbuildings and endless fences and herds of white-and-red cattle everywhere.

"The ranch?" she asked, excited.

"The ranch." He chuckled at her expression as he pulled off the main highway onto the winding dirt road. "Like it?"

"Oh, I love it," she said softly, drinking in the lush greens and the wildflowers that seemed to be everywhere. "Those are sunflowers!" she exclaimed.

"You'll find a lot of unfamiliar vegetation," he said. "We don't have sea grapes and palms out here. We have water oaks and hickory trees.... Of course, we have some fascinating animals here, too. I doubt you've ever seen a moose."

"I can hardly wait."

"You shouldn't be this enthusiastic," he murmured dryly, remembering how much Bess had hated the ranch when she and Bobby married. Of course, Bess had grown up in dirt-poor surroundings, and he supposed she'd had her fill of roughing it. She'd probably longed for something completely different, more refined. But Bobby, like King, had loved the plains, loved walking the hills in search of arrowheads—one of King's favorite childhood pastimes. "You're a city girl, remember?"

"I'm a country girl," she argued. "Just because I work near Miami doesn't make me citified. I like wide open spaces, like the beach and hills. Can I go walking when I feel like it, or are there..."

"Wild Indians?" he suggested with a wicked grin.

She hit him. "Wolves," she replied.

"Only this one," he murmured, winking at her.

She gave up, shaking her head. She didn't remember the reason he'd brought her here. The real reason. He still wanted her. It was in his eyes, in the way he smiled at her. And Bess was somewhere nearby....

"Where does Bobby live?" she asked suddenly.

The smile left his face. "There." He indicated a modern split-level house in the distance. "Almost in Jack's Corner. Bess used to spend a lot of time in Oklahoma City, but Bobby said she's started getting interested in local society." He frowned. "Too bad it's only tea parties and such. She sure could do a lot of social work if she had a mind to."

He drove the Lincoln up to the front steps, and Elissa sighed over the big green rocking chairs and the porch swing. "I love it!" She grinned. "Can we sit in the swing?"

"Presently," he promised, climbing out to open her door and help her, with old-world courtesy, to the ground.

The screen door swung open, and a middle-aged woman stomped onto the porch. Margaret Floyd, the housekeeper, was a big, buxom woman in her sixties with white hair and dark eyes and a mean-looking expression.

"Well, it's about time," she said, parking her hands on her broad hips. She was wearing a pale-yellow print housedress with purple bedroom shoes, and a splattered white apron hugged her ample middle. "You're an hour late.

What did you do, get hijacked on the way back? I've ruined dinner, you'll be glad to know, and who's that?''

Elissa was being dragged up the steps and pushed forward like a shield before she had time to catch her breath.

"This is Elissa Dean," King said, holding her there firmly, even though she wasn't struggling.

"Well, glory be!" Margaret's broad face brightened like a sunflower. "Finally!"

She rushed forward, and Elissa found herself engulfed in the smell of flour and apples.

"I thought he'd never get enough sense to bring you home," Margaret gushed. "Idiot, chasing after them stupid city women." She glared at King before turning back to Elissa. "You look like a nice girl. He says you still live at home," she added with unashamed curiosity.

"Well, yes," Elissa stammered. "My folks wouldn't have it any other way."

Margaret looked as if all her prayers had been answered. "Lordy, child, do come in and let me feed you. I've got a delicious pot roast, even if I do say so myself, and a pan of homemade rolls, and I baked him an apple pie."

King went back to get the luggage, muttering things it was just as well Margaret didn't actually hear. Margaret was a wonderful cook, had a mind like a steel trap and didn't feel the least bashful about asking the most intimate kind of questions.

King finally ran her off so they could eat their meal in peace. Elissa's face was beet red by then, and he looked a bit put out himself. Elissa couldn't know that over the years, only Bess had ever been afforded such courteous treatment by the housekeeper. Margaret had always found not so subtle ways of showing her disapproval for the type of woman King had entertained so frequently in his younger days. Bess had been different, because Margaret knew her background and was frankly sorry for her.

"It's a lovely meal," Elissa said finally.

"Lovely," he muttered.

She didn't attempt conversation again. She finished the food and allowed Margaret to whisk her upstairs to unpack.

King was called out the minute he left the supper table to attend to sixty things the foreman—Ben Floyd, Margaret's husband—hadn't been able to, despite neighbor Blake Donavan's help.

Elissa found herself alone after Margaret went to her own small house below the stables, and when King didn't come back by midnight, she went to bed. Her first day on the ranch had been an experience.

The next morning, she awoke to strange noises. Cattle lowing. A rooster crowing. The barking of a dog. Clatter from downstairs. She sat up in bed with a lazy yawn and drank in the sweet, clean country air. It wasn't so far removed from the Florida coast, after all. Country was country, except for the noises.

She got up and dressed in jeans and a short-sleeved blouse, feeling as summery as the weather. She left her hair down and her face clear of makeup.

Downstairs, King was sitting at the breakfast table with a brooding look. But it wasn't the King she'd become accustomed to. This was a Westerner with a capital *W*. She stood stock-still in the doorway, just staring.

From his faded jeans and dusty boots up over a blue-and-white Western shirt to his dark hair, he was a different man. It wasn't only the clothing; it was something in his face. A different look. A naturalness. A man in his native setting.

He looked up from his newspaper and cocked an eyebrow. "Well? Aren't you hungry?"

"Of course." She sat down beside him, her eyes curious.

"You've seen me in jeans before," he reminded her, amused at her expression.

"You never looked like this before," she faltered. Her eyes searched his.

He winked at her. "Did you sleep well?"

"Beautifully," she sighed. "How about you?"

"When I finally got to sleep," he muttered darkly, "it was soundly. Ben had five hours' work waiting."

"Wasn't some neighbor supposed to be watching things for you?"

"He was, and he did," came a deep, amused voice from the doorway, "but only Kingston can sign Kingston's name to his checks."

Elissa turned to find the voice. The man she saw made her shiver. He looked dangerous, a wild man with unruly black hair and pale-green eyes set in lashes as thick and black as his eyebrows. He was lithe and lean and sported a scar down one cheek and a nose that looked to have been broken once too often. Somehow he didn't look like the kind of man King would call a friend, and Elissa wondered how much else there was to learn about the enigmatic man she'd fallen in love with.

"Blake Donavan," King introduced him. "This is my houseguest, Elissa Dean."

"I'm glad to meet you, Mr. Donavan," she said hesitantly.

He gave her an indifferent appraisal and nodded. "Same here." He turned his attention to King. "If you've got everything you need, I'll head back home. I've got those damned lawyers waiting. At least this time it's for something productive. My signature goes on a document, and the suit's settled once and for all."

King lifted his coffee cup. "I hear Meredith Calhoun just won an award for her latest book."

The green eyes kindled, and the lean face seemed to close up. Obviously this writer, whoever she was, was a touchy subject for Blake Donavan, Elissa noted. Had King brought up the name deliberately? she wondered.

"I've got work to do," Donavan said tersely. "See you, Roper. Miss Dean," he added, touching the brim of his hat, and was gone.

"Who's Meredith Calhoun?" Elissa whispered, mindful of the open door.

King sighed. "That's a long story," he replied, apparently unwilling to delve into it.

"He's a hard-looking man," she ventured.

"Pure diamond," he agreed, "and it goes straight through. If he looks hard, it's because life made him hard. He was illegitimate, and his mother died in childbirth. He was taken in by a crusty old uncle who adopted him and gave him his name. The uncle died last year, and Donavan's been in a hell of a court battle for the property ever since."

"I can see why he won," she remarked, shivering slightly and wondering anew at King's ready compassion for life's unfortunates. Of course, that compassion was what had made him so vulnerable to Bess.... "He's younger than you, isn't he?" she said weakly, dragging her thoughts back to the present.

His dark eyes narrowed on her face. "Yes. Eight years. He's almost thirty-two. Why? Does he appeal to you?"

She blinked. That sounded amazingly like jealousy. Why on earth should he feel possessive about her when it was Bess he loved?

Without waiting for her reply—besides, she was too stunned and confused to offer one—he got to his feet. "I've got a full day's work ahead of me."

"Not in your office, I gather?" she fished.

"On my ranch," he said, leaning down to press a hard, warm kiss on her parted lips. "This is how I relax, tidbit— by keeping busy. Manual labor built this ranch."

"You look like a cowboy," she mused, surprised by the ardent kiss.

"I am a cowboy," he replied, searching her blue eyes. "I can travel first-class and buy damned near anything I want, but what I like best is a horse under me and open land around me and a night sky to sleep under."

"Do you?" She reached up to him, and amazingly, he came to her, letting her have his mouth. She kissed him warmly and was stunned by the softness of his lips, by his eager participation in a caress that had nothing to do with sex.

"Want to come see the calves later?" he asked as he lifted his head. "If you're good, I'll even let you pet one."

"Yes, I'd like to," she said, smiling lazily.

He drew in a slow, pleased breath as his eyes drank in her lovely face. "Fairy face," he whispered. He bent again, brushing her mouth with his. "I'll see you at lunch. Don't let Margaret talk you to death."

"I like Margaret," she murmured.

"Margaret likes you, too, baby doll," Margaret said from the doorway with a platter of eggs in her hand. She grinned toothily at King. "You lucky man, you."

King actually flushed. "I've got work to do," he mumbled, and he left them both there, pulling his hat down over his eyes with a jerk as he strode noisily from the room.

"Only walks that way when I've annoyed him," Margaret assured her, grinning even wider. "But you're the first girl he's brought home to me to visit in a long, long time, so I reckon he's in pretty deep. But you watch him; he's no choirboy. He can be right dangerous in full pursuit."

Elissa burst out laughing. "Oh, Margaret, you're a jewel," she said, and meant it. "He doesn't love me, you know. I'm just his friend, that's all."

Margaret nodded as she sat down. "That's right, and I'm a Halloween pumpkin," she agreed. She helped herself to a cup of coffee and folded her hefty forearms on the table. She stared straight at Elissa. "Now, tell me about yourself. I hear you design clothes."

It was like the Spanish Inquisition. By the time Elissa was allowed to escape and go exploring around the house, Margaret knew her favorite perfume, her entire family history—she'd hooted with delight upon learning King had brought home a minister's daughter—and as much as possible of her potential future.

The ranch itself was a new experience. There were well-kept stables housing beautiful Appaloosas, cattle everywhere and a bull who seemed to have his own building and a full-time caretaker. He was red and white, like most of the cattle, and as big as a house. When King came home at lunchtime, he found her at the barn, staring at the creature.

"His name is King's Pride 4120," he informed her smugly, hands in his pockets. "He's out of the foundation herd of Herefords Bobby's grandfather began here, but I've improved the strain with selective breeding."

"Why does he have a number?" she asked. "Has he been arrested or something?"

"That gets complicated." He threw an affectionate arm around her shoulders and led her back to the house, explaining things like embryo transplants and daily weight-gain ratios and all the intricacies of breeding superior beef cattle. The technical information rattled around in Elissa's head like marbles, but it was fascinating all the same.

"Margaret's making beef-salad sandwiches for lunch," she told him on the front porch, where the big green swing and several rocking chairs faced the open plains.

"How much has she dragged out of you so far?" he asked with a raised eyebrow and a dry smile.

"Before or after she got to the color of my underwear?" She laughed.

He just shook his head.

Lunch was quiet. Margaret went off to listen to the news while she worked in the kitchen, and King didn't seem inclined to talk. Afterward, he saddled a horse for her with the ease of long practice and helped her into the saddle. This, at least, was familiar; they'd gone riding together in Jamaica several times over the past two years. She glanced at him under the brim of her borrowed straw hat, thinking how everything about him was familiar to her and yet subtly different these days.

He caught her glance and grinned. "Remember the day we rode down the beach hell-for-leather, and you fell off in the surf?"

"I'm holding on tight this time," she retorted, wrapping the reins around her hand. "Lead on, cowboy; you won't lose me."

"Let's see."

He took off, nudging his Appaloosa gelding to a quick lead. She followed on her mare, laughing delightedly at the open land and his company and the sunny afternoon.

The calves were Herefords, and not newborn as she'd expected. The calves started coming in February and March, he told her, to coincide with his breeding program. They were fattened up and then sold when they reached the desired weight.

"It's so sad to think of eating them," she mused while she scratched a white-topknotted head above soulful brown eyes. "Isn't he cute?"

He leaned against the fence post, his hat pushed back, his eyes watchful. "They tell stories about the cattle drives in the old days and how close the cattle got to their drovers. They say that sometimes the cowboys had to actually go with the cattle into the abbatoirs, to keep them from stampeding. They bawled when the drovers started to leave them."

Tears sprang to her eyes. She was vaguely embarrassed at her sentimentality and tried to hide her reaction, but he saw her tears. He caught her gently by the shoulders, turning her. He bent, lifting her into his arms, and carried her back to the horses.

"I'm sorry," she whispered.

"You soft-hearted little greenhorn," he whispered back, and he smiled as he brought his mouth with exquisite tenderness to hers.

He'd meant it to be a sweet, comforting gesture, but her mouth opened beneath his, and his breath stopped in his throat. He hesitated, but only for a second. Then he carried her away from the horses and laid her down in the tall buffalo grass, his lean body settling completely over her.

"King!" she gasped.

"Elissa," he breathed huskily. He kissed her hungrily, giving in to the aching need, the long nights of wanting her. He reached under her to catch her hips and drag them lazily against his, letting her feel the evidence of his need. And for long, exquisite moments, they enjoyed the touch and taste and feel for each other.

Then, when it was almost too much, he groaned and rolled onto his back. Not since his teens had he felt so damned helpless to control himself. And she could see how much she aroused him.

She sat up, her eyes like saucers, and he held her rapt gaze.

"This never happens to me," he whispered, his voice deep and husky and gruff. "Never this quick or this completely with any woman but you, damn it."

Her lips parted on a smile as she looked at him, not with triumph but with love. "Do you mind if that makes me proud?" she asked softly.

He drew in an unsteady breath. "I guess not." He sat up, bending over his upraised knees. "I can't imagine how I've lasted this long."

She touched his hand where it rested on his knee. "I'm sorry," she said softly, searching the dark, tormented eyes that met hers. "But it pleases me that even if you don't love me, at least you want me."

He brought her hand to his mouth. "Do you want me to love you?" he asked quietly. "Because that may come in time. Marry me, Elissa."

She lowered her eyes to his hand. "I'll have to think about it," she said finally, biting her tongue to keep from screaming yes. She had to be reasonable. She couldn't let her love for him influence her; she had to think of what was best for him, too, since obviously he wasn't thinking at all.

His fingers tightened. He started to speak and then seemed to decide against it. "All right."

She looked up. "Does Bobby know we're here?"

"Yes," he said finally. "I called him a few hours ago. Bess is in Oklahoma City until tomorrow morning. He invited us to go riding with them."

"When?"

"Tomorrow afternoon." He tilted her face up. "Don't decide now. You've got one hell of a big decision to work up to by bedtime."

Her lips trembled. "I . . . I care for you," she whispered.

His hand touched her cheek, and he wished he could read her mind. He felt guilty and uncertain, but he cared for her, too, in his way. "Then marry me," he said, feeling oddly certain that it would be the right thing for them both. "Say yes."

She managed a quiet sigh. Logic went out the window. "Yes."

He stared into her eyes for a long time, feeling electricity arc between them. He wanted her. He was fond of her. She cared for him. It would be enough. And it would be a final, permanent barrier between him and Bess.

He bent to her mouth and kissed her very gently before he helped her to her feet and back into the saddle. He didn't say another word all the way home.

Nine

Elissa spent the afternoon helping Margaret in the kitchen. King had gone out again, presumably to finish his ranch work. Margaret kept throwing the younger woman speaking glances, and Elissa knew she must look troubled.

"Out with it," Margaret said finally. "What's wrong?"

"He wants to marry me," Elissa replied, scouring a pan they'd used to fry steak for lunch.

"Halleluja!"

"It isn't that simple," she said with a rueful smile. She turned back to the pan. "He doesn't love me."

"Men don't know what love is until they're in too deep to climb out," Margaret observed, chuckling. "I've seen how he looks at you. There's enough there to build on—you mark my words."

Elissa tingled. Yes, he did look at her as if she were a sumptuous dessert. But there was still Bess to consider. She sighed.

"Don't worry about it," the older woman coaxed. "Just say yes, and I'll take care of everything. Let's see, invitations and the reception, and champagne and hors d'oeuvres," she murmured.

Elissa didn't say anything else. She was too worried.

They sat down to supper alone, and after cleaning up, Margaret finally went home, bubbling with happiness. Elissa arranged a plate for King and covered it, and she was just wiping up a spill on the floor when King walked in the back door.

He looked at little dusty and very tired. He studied her from under the wide brim of his Stetson, taking in the picture she made in a loose gold-and-white caftan, kneeling there against the spotless cream linoleum.

"You're a picture, do you know it?" he mused. "All that long, sexy hair and big blue eyes, and your tan looks pretty good with white and gold."

She stood up, smiling. "You look like a cowboy," she replied.

His eyebrows arched. "Is that a compliment or a criticism?"

She lowered her eyes shyly. "I like cowboys."

"Where's Margaret?"

"Gone home. I've fixed you a plate, if you're hungry."

He looked faintly sheepish for a minute, steadying his dusty boots. "Well, Jim was up at the cow camp with us," he began. "Jim's the cook when we're working. He rustled up a pot of chili and some tortillas and a pudding that I expect to dream about for days." He cocked his head at her. "Don't tell Margaret, will you? I'll get burned biscuits for a week if she finds out. Could you dispose of that plateful of stuff without her knowing?"

She laughed delightfully. "Of course."

"I'll be down directly, once I clean up, and I'll thank you properly," he murmured, lowering his voice an octave.

She felt her heart skip at the look in his dark eyes as he went by her. He winked on his way into the hall, and she watched him go, feeling strangely quiet and contented yet delirious with anticipation.

He paused on the middle step and looked down at her. "How about making some coffee?" he asked. "I'll come back down and we'll share a pot while we talk."

His eyes fell to her body and lingered. She felt weak in the knees. He wanted more than just talk, and she knew it. They were so much on the same wavelength that she could almost feel him breathing.

"I'll do that," she said, her voice husky.

He nodded. His eyes smiled. "And I could do with a piece of cake, if there's any left," he added.

"There's enough. I'll slice it. Don't drown in the shower," she teased.

"I can swim." He grinned and continued up the stairs.

Elissa made coffee and carried the silver service into the living room, curling up on the sofa to wait for him. Minutes later he joined her, dressed in clean denims and a half-unbuttoned blue-check shirt. His hair was damp, and he smelled of soap and spicy cologne. Elissa could hardly take her eyes off him as he eased his tall, powerful frame down on the sofa beside her.

"I'll pour," she said. She sounded, and was, flustered. To disguise it, she moved to the floor in front of the coffee table so that she was just in front of him. It was all she could do to get the coffee out of the heavy silver pot into the white china cups.

"You're nervous. Why?" he asked quietly.

She laughed. "I don't know."

He reached down, turning her so that she was kneeling between his legs. His fingers traced her flushed cheeks, and his eyes were steady on hers. Everything she felt was in her face—it was like reading a book—and his reaction to that blatant adoration shocked him. He felt a surge of possession strong enough to knock the breath out of him, and his body was suddenly, achingly hungry for hers. Not for sex alone but for something more. He frowned. He'd never felt that need before, not with any woman. He wanted to...to join with Elissa. To know her in every way there was.

He felt oddly young as he bent toward her, and the first touch of his mouth against her soft one was tentative. He drank in the floral scent of her, drowned in her shy, eager response. It was always like this with her, like flying, like bubbles in champagne. She was his from the moment he touched her. But now it felt as if he belonged to her, as well.

With a long, aching sigh, he brought her up against him, easing her onto his lap as he deepened the slow, tender kiss. She felt his kiss with wonder, because it had never been like this before. She relaxed into him, looping her arms around his neck, her mouth parting, opening under the sweet ardor of his.

She felt his hands at her waist, tracing her rib cage, then delicately touching the soft contours of her breasts. Under the caftan she wore only pale-yellow briefs, and when he felt her skin so close, his breath caught.

Her body began to tremble as he stroked it, his fingers deft and sure and faintly insistent. His mouth hardened on hers, and her ears were filled with the harsh quickness of his breathing and her own faint gasps when he touched her more intimately.

Her soft blue eyes looked up into his when he lifted his head, and she saw a strange expression there. "What is it?" she whispered unsteadily.

He watched his fingers tracing her breasts, watched the involuntarily movement of her body at the pleasure he gave her. "I want you," he breathed. "But not...like I've ever wanted anyone else." His dark eyes went back to hers. "I want to join your body to mine. I want oneness...."

Her lips parted. "Yes." Even as she thought the word, she said it, because this might be the only time. She might lose him, but this once she could belong to him. He knew she was a virgin. It would be special. It would be everything.

She slid the zipper of the caftan down to her waist, and his chest rose sharply. He searched her eyes for a long moment before he eased the fabric out of the way and looked at her. After a moment, he bent, and his lips began to touch her in reverent adoration. Her breasts, her belly and her hips burned under his mouth. She moved helplessly as he touched her in ways he never had, and long before he eased her out of her caftan and briefs, she was lost.

She moaned when he moved away long enough to strip off his own clothing, his eyes dark and sensual and full of desire. There was a faint tremor in his powerful body as he sat back down on the sofa and eased her gently over him, so that she was sitting facing him. She gasped at the first touch of skin against skin, light against dark, hard muscle against softness.

"There's nothing to be afraid of," he whispered, brushing her body in agonizingly slow movements against his, her breasts just barely touching him, her hips trembling against his blatant masculinity.

Her hands gripped his hard arms, and she leaned her forehead against his chest so that he wouldn't see the fear. "Is it going to hurt?" she whispered.

"It's going to be beautiful," he whispered back, his hands on her hips. "Give me your mouth."

She lifted her face and saw the soft affection in his eyes. Her heart was his. She loved him so. It was magic, the way it felt, to be this way with him, to be intimate with him. Her mind was beyond right and wrong, in thrall to the budding demands of her own womanhood.

His hands explored her waist and hips, gently caressing, softly arousing. He moved her hips against his, and she bit back a moan. She clung to him, astounded by what was happening.

"Oh, King," she whispered achingly, lifting her eyes.

He eased her upward then, holding her gaze while he positioned her hips against his. His face was that of a stranger, utterly sensual, slightly threatening, but there was something in his dark eyes that held her spellbound. He bent, his breath mingling with hers as he brushed his mouth over hers in lazy, comforting sweeps that eased her fear.

While his lips toyed with hers, his hands were learning the silken contours of her body. He teased her breasts, nudging their hardened tips, making her tremble with the sensations he aroused. He nipped her lower lip and trailed his mouth over her throat, her shoulders and, finally, the soft swell of her breasts.

She could hardly breathe. She held his arms for support, her eyes closed, the air cool at her back. He moved then, and she felt the sudden contact with his thighs, the ripple of muscles as he probed her softly. She gasped, looking up, her breath stopped in her throat.

He moved against her, very slowly, holding her eyes. His hands made their way to her hips, moving her against him in a slow, lazy, arousing rhythm. She didn't understand what was happening to her. She felt her body begin to tremble, and she gasped when he increased the gentle rise and fall of his hips against her. She clutched at him, overwhelmed by the intimacy of the gesture.

"King...sitting up?" she gasped, her voice scarcely recognizable to her own ears.

"Shh," he whispered, lowering his mouth over hers in delicious teasing motions. "Just relax, little one. I wouldn't hurt a hair on your sweet head for all the cows in Texas."

"But...like this?"

He laughed gently, even though his body was shuddering with his need of her. He looked down at her taut breasts and deliberately pressed his hard, hair-roughened chest against them. She moaned, and the sound fired his blood.

"Are you going to get noisy?" he whispered into her mouth. "I won't mind." He bit her lower lip delicately while one hand teased her swollen breast and moved down slowly to her hips, her thighs, and into a sudden, wildly shocking intimacy that she instinctively protested. But after a minute, when her body demanded that she let him do it, she gave in and held on, crying out softly at the delicious pleasure he was giving her. She felt tears sting her eyes and run down into her mouth.

He tasted them and lifted his head to watch her fevered eyes, her flushed face, while he savored her sweet body. "It won't be hard for you," he whispered, and he shifted, just a little, holding her hips. "It won't be hard at all. Don't tense up. I'm going to show you the mystery, Elissa. I'm going to make a woman of you now."

She felt him arch slightly, and her lips parted on a soft gasp. She looked into his eyes, frightened at the first burning stab of sensation.

His hands framed her face as he moved again, and she jerked a little. "Another few seconds," he whispered, his voice soft and slow and intimate. He smiled. "Relax for me. It won't ever hurt again, I promise," he breathed brokenly, his hands bringing her down to him.

He kissed her softly as he took her completely, and her nails bit into him. She started to stiffen, but she bit her lip and laid her forehead against his broad, damp chest and forced her body to admit him. There was only a small stab of pain, and then she sighed in relief.

His hands moved on her, stroking her, doing impossible things, moving her, shifting her. He bent to her mouth again, probing it with his tongue. He took it, and his hips began to move, and she felt a savage ripple of pleasure that took her by surprise. Surely, she thought dazedly, she'd only imagined it. But he moved, and it came again. And again. She bit his shoulder, shuddering. He shuddered, too, and she felt his body surge powerfully.

He lifted his mouth just enough to look at her. "Exquisite," he whispered, studying her. "That expression, wild and tortured, as if I were hurting you. But I'm not, am I?"

"No," she whispered. His hand moved, and she cried out, biting her lip.

"Don't stop yourself," he gasped as he increased his rhythm, his eyes stormy and dark. "There's no one to hear you. Let it out. Make noise," he whispered. "Make as much noise as you want."

His hands bit into her thighs, holding her down to him. Her eyes dilated, because she'd never expected that it would be like this. Her head fell back, and she gasped as he arched under her. His face was a mask of passion, tight and flushed, his eyes black as night and glittering, exultant.

She cried out, and her fingers bit into his shoulders as she shuddered with unexpected, total completion, his name a hoarse sound torn from her throat.

He felt her convulse, stunned that it should happen for her the first time. And then he felt the familiar stab of fulfillment racking him, and he cried out her name over and over.

A long time later she wafted back to earth. Under her, his body was damp and shuddering in the aftermath, his hands protective now, soothing, tender. He lifted his face to hers and began to kiss her, his hard mouth so tender and cherishing that she wanted to cry. He whispered her name over and over again, his voice awed. He'd never experienced anything like this in his life. With Elissa, he'd attained heights he hadn't touched before. Whatever this was, it wasn't simply sex.

His body still trembling, he kissed her closed eyes warmly and then her face again, in soft, searching caresses. She felt loved, cherished, and she smiled against his damp throat.

He nipped her ear. "I felt it happen to you," he murmured. "It almost never does the first time."

"My body didn't know. I'll make sure I tell it."

"Imp," he drawled. He looked into her eyes and shifted his hips, his eyes hot and wicked when she gasped. "Shocking, isn't it?" he whispered. And then his gaze softened, and his smile faded. "I hope you aren't having second thoughts," he said quietly.

She opened her mouth to tell him that she wasn't protected, but his opened against it, and his hips rose and fell, and the pleasure came stabbing back in a rhythm that was already familiar.

"Angel face," he whispered softly. "I've dreamed about this for so long, about how it would be with you. It was beyond my wildest dreams. It was perfection," he breathed, touching her face reverently. "My God, it's never been like that for me. Never."

She stared at his hair-roughened chest and touched it tentatively, liking the feel under her fingers. He stiffened a little, and she smiled at him. "You're very good at this," she said shyly, wondering how many women there had been before her. The thought disturbed her a little, and her conscience was twinging. He didn't love her, she knew, but she loved him. Was that reason enough to covet this oneness with him? This one night out of a lifetime, when she could lie in his arms and pretend that he loved her? She refused to think. She leaned forward and kissed his chest softly. "You'll have to show me what to do to make it good for you," she whispered.

"The mind boggles," he whispered back, sliding his mouth softly over hers. "Come on. We'll have a shower, and then we'll go to bed." He lifted his head, searching her eyes. "If you still want to."

She returned that intent look. "I want to," she assured him.

He carried their things upstairs to his bedroom and led her into the shower. For the next few minutes they soaped and explored each other and kissed until her mouth was swollen and his body was making new and urgent demands.

"I'm not protected," she whispered as he laid her down on the bed. "I should have told you before."

"I don't give a damn," he breathed. He was on fire for her, burning. Consequences didn't seem to matter anymore, and they were engaged, so what the hell. "A baby wouldn't be the end of my world or yours."

"How would you make love to me if you wanted a baby?" she whispered, her eyes soft with love.

He smiled as he brushed her mouth with his. "Very much as I did downstairs," he murmured against her lips. "As if you were innocent all over again. We'd be exquisitely tender with each other, like two people desperately in love. Like...this."

It was tender. And profound. He drew it out, exploring her body like some delicate treasure that might break with a harsh breath. Even when he began to take her, it was still gentle, their eyes openly cherishing each other, their voices hushed. When the tide came and washed them into the blinding heat of fulfillment, they were still looking into each other's eyes, and it was a gentle violence, rocking them with exquisitely tender shudders and warm convulsions that were even more beautiful than those of wild passion.

When it was over, she cried helplessly, and he held her, kissing away the tears, cradling her against his damp body.

"You make it so profound," he whispered shakily. "It isn't even physical with you, it's a thing so much of the spirit that it makes me tremble. I never dreamed of such fulfillment."

"You make love beautifully," she breathed.

"So do you, baby." He curled her into his body with a weary sigh. "I want to sleep with you, Elissa. I never want to let go of you."

She cuddled close to him, savoring his strength, feeling secure and adored and totally fulfilled. At the back of her mind, a tiny voice nagged that it wasn't right or proper, but she was too tired to listen.

"Don't hate me," he breathed.

"How could I?"

"I took you out of wedlock."

"I offered myself."

"Did you? Or did I simply back you into a corner and take the choice away from you?" He lifted his head to search her eyes. "Will you mind if I made you pregnant?"

"There probably wasn't much risk," she murmured shyly.

"The way we made love that last time, there was most definitely a risk," he said.

She nuzzled her face against him. "Will you hate me if that happens?"

"Never."

"Babies can create problems."

His arms tightened. "Babies are little tiny breathing miracles. Now shut up and go to sleep. I'm so tired, it's all I can do to breathe, you insatiable little witch."

"*I'm* insatiable?" she burst out.

He only grinned and folded her closer. "Go to sleep. If you're able, I'll make love to you again when we wake up."

She sighed. "What a delicious incentive to sleep."

"I thought so, too."

It seemed like no time at all before the sounds of farm equipment outside the window brought her eyes open. She looked down at King, smiling at his nudity, at the vulnerability of his powerful body in sleep.

"It's morning," she whispered in his ear.

"Is it?" he whispered back, smiling. He opened his eyes and reached for her, his intentions obvious. "Are you up to this?" he asked solicitously.

She pressed down against him. "I want you," she whispered before bringing her mouth to his.

He took a long time with her, despite his overpowering hunger, and it was late morning before he was satisfied enough to get up. He stretched grandly and looked down at her sprawled facedown on the bed.

"You miracle, you," he breathed. "Roll over. I want to look at you while I dress."

She did, smiling at him, watching him open drawers and the closet and get into jeans and a chambray shirt. "It's even exciting to watch you put clothes on," she confessed, laughing.

"I'd rather watch you with yours off, angel," he murmured, bending to brush hungry kisses on her breasts. "I want you all the time, lately. It's all I can do to stop." He lifted his head, searching her eyes. "You flinched a little that last time," he said gently. "It wasn't comfortable, and you should have told me in time. I'll leave you alone until you're sure it won't be an ordeal instead of a pleasure."

"You're very perceptive," she murmured.

"You're very generous," he whispered. "So eager to please me, to put my desire first. But that isn't what I want. It gives me no pleasure unless you share it."

"Oh, but I want to give you everything, to make it sweet for you," she said fervently. "I don't care what I feel—"

He stopped her tirade with his mouth, smiling against it. "*I* care. Come on downstairs when you're dressed, and I'll take you for a nice, comfortable ride in the Lincoln. No horseback riding just yet." He grinned, and she flushed.

"Okay."

He lifted her hand to his lips, studying her over it. An innocent, and with all her inhibitions, and yet she'd given herself to him with wild abandon. She cared more than a little; he was almost sure she loved him. That thought was sweetly disturbing. Could she? He looked at her hungrily. All night, and still he wanted her. She was under his skin, driving him mad. Bess and his problems with her had faded to insignificance. Whatever he and Elissa had, it was something far removed from lust or infatuation. He wanted to take care of her, to be there when she cried. He sighed softly. What was he going to do about Bess? Or did he need to do anything, now that he was marrying Elissa? He thought about marrying Elissa and smiled slowly. She'd be in his bed every night, making magic with him. His chest began to swell.

She saw that look and smiled at him. "Don't feel guilty," she whispered. "I don't."

"Don't you?" he asked quietly.

"Not in the least," she said, ignoring her conscience.

"Anyway, I wasn't thinking about guilt," he confessed. "I was wondering if you loved me," he added bluntly, watching her flush. "Somehow, I don't think you'd be able to give yourself to a man you didn't love. You're not the type." He touched her cheek, teasing her face up to his. "Don't hide it," he whispered, finding the evidence of love in her face wildly pleasing, exciting. His breath caught in his throat, and he wondered why it should suddenly matter so much that she loved him. "That was why you were so uninhibited, wasn't it?" he asked slowly. "That was why I gave you pleasure the first time. And you did enjoy it."

"More than you'll ever know," she confessed. "Do you mind?"

He shook his head. "You're very special to me."

"Even when we aren't lovers anymore," she began, her eyes wide and worried, "will you still be my friend?"

That hurt. He sat down and lifted her across his knees, cuddling her close. "My God," he ground out, his arms wrapped tightly around her. "You little fool. You don't have some crazy idea that I was just satisfying a whim last night, do you?"

"I hoped it wasn't that."

"I'm going to marry you," he whispered. "This isn't a one-night stand. For God's sake, Elissa, you're part of me now."

She trembled a little at the urgency in his voice, at his warmth and fervency. She turned her mouth against his throat and kissed him. "Thank you," she said.

"I don't want thanks." He lifted his head and looked into her eyes, his expression both thrilling and puzzling. His dark gaze went over her slowly, lingering on her breasts. "I'm more old-fashioned than I realized," he said unexpectedly. "If you ever let another man touch you like I did, I'd break his neck!"

"Well!" she gasped, but his mouth covered hers fiercely, blotting out the world.

"You're my woman," he whispered against her responsive lips. "You belong to me. We're going to get married and enjoy each other for the next eighty years or so."

Her arms linked around his neck, and she savored the pressure of his mouth for a long, spinning minute until he finally satisfied his hunger and lifted his head.

"Get dressed," he whispered. "I can't take much more of that without laying you down and ravishing you again."

She smiled softly. "I adore you."

"I adore you," he whispered. He smiled at her, new to possession, new to that look in her eyes, that total fulfillment his loving had given her. It made him proud that he could fulfill her, that he'd done it her first time.

"You look smug," she mentioned.

He dumped her onto the bed, looming over her to press a hard kiss on her mouth. "I feel smug. Now get up."

"Yes, your worship."

He glanced at her on his way out the door and smiled again as he closed it behind him. He couldn't remember a time in his life when he'd felt so pleased with himself, so satiated with happiness that he felt as if he could do anything.

She dressed quickly, taking time to sneak down the hall to her room and mess up her bed—only to find that he'd already done it. She smiled to herself as she went downstairs, wrapped in the sweet illusion of loving and being loved.

He was sipping coffee when she got to the kitchen, and his eyes when they met hers were dark with acquisition. His chin rose, all male arrogance in the smile he gave her. His eyes ran down her body with remembered possession, and they kindled like dusky fires.

She tingled all over as she joined him, her mouth softening at his welcoming kiss.

"Here," he whispered.

She opened her eyes to find him sliding a solitary emerald onto her ring finger. It was in a delicate antique filigree setting, and a perfect fit. She caught her breath, her eyes searching, questioning his.

"It belonged to my grandmother," he said, his face solemn. "You can give it to our eldest son...."

"King." Tears fell like rain from her eyes. She went into his arms, trembling all over. If only she could stop wondering if it might be guilt and a sense of responsibility that had led to this. She knew he didn't love her, although he was fond of her and he did enjoy her body. But maybe in time he might learn to love her. She clung to him. "I love you so much," she said shakily, her eyes closed so that she missed the delight on his dark face. "So much."

He held her, his expression one of contentment, rocking her softly against him. God, she was soft. Sweet. Deliciously female. She smelled of flowers, and he wanted to hold her all day. She felt just right in his arms. He smiled, closing his eyes.

"Now, ain't that pretty?" Margaret sighed from the doorway, smiling benevolently at both of them.

"Look," Elissa said tearfully, sitting on King's lap to extend her slender finger with the emerald ring on it.

"Glory be!" Margaret exclaimed. "We really are having a wedding!"

"Looks like it, doesn't it?" King said affectionately.

"I'll go tell Ben." Margaret grinned and walked away.

Elissa was just starting to speak when the phone rang.

"I'll get it," he said as he set her on her feet. He walked into the hall and picked up the receiver, listened for a minute and took a sharp breath. "What the hell was he doing on it in the first place?" he demanded. "No, honey, don't, don't. I'm sorry. God, I'm sorry. Listen, sweetheart, you just sit tight, you hear? I'll be right there. Everything will be all right. I'm on my way."

He hung up and dug into his pocket for his car keys. "Bobby's been thrown from a horse," he said tersely. "Bess came in last night, and they went riding together this morning. He's got a concussion and a broken leg, at least. I'll have to go to the hospital, honey. Bess was pretty upset. She needs me."

Elissa just sat there, stunned, as he turned away without another word. She watched him rush out the door, on his way to Bess, without a backward glance toward the woman he'd just asked to marry him. She closed her eyes, feeling the tears start. If this was a glimpse of the future, she'd just looked straight into hell.

Ten

Margaret came back minutes later to find Elissa cupping her hands around a cup of cold coffee, a look of utter defeat on her face.

"Where's he gone?" the older woman asked curtly.

"Bobby was thrown from a horse," Elissa said quickly, looking up. "He's got a broken leg and a concussion. King's gone to the hospital."

Margaret whistled. "I knew it would happen one day." She shook her head. "Bobby isn't a rider, for all he keeps trying. Will he be all right?"

"Bess didn't say, apparently," she faltered.

The older woman sat down, staring at Elissa. "That young madam has too much time on her hands and not enough husband," she said bluntly. "I've known both them boys for a long time—watched them fuss and fight and grow into men. Bobby's too eaten up trying to compete with his half brother to be the man he could be. All business, even when he comes to dinner over here. Bess sits there watching him so sadly, and he doesn't see her at all. I understand why he's doing it, mind you, but Bess isn't the kind of woman a man should treat that way. God knows she had a hard enough life, what with her family."

Margaret was good for half an hour on that subject. By the time she got through the alcoholic father and eternally pregnant mother and the abject poverty Bess had grown up in, Elissa felt sorrier for the blonde than she'd ever dreamed she could. But King had gone running when Bess needed him, and that fact stood out above all the rest. Was he simply sorry for Bess and protective of her, or was it something more?

"You don't mind that he went to see about Bobby?" Margaret asked suddenly.

"Oh, heavens, no!" Elissa said. "I would have gone, too, if he'd asked me." She shrugged, biting back tears. "I guess he was thinking that Bess would need some support."

Margaret's eyes narrowed. "Bess loves Bobby," she said quietly. "Sometimes she may flirt with other men, but that's all it ever is. And Kingston asked you to marry him, didn't he?"

"Yes, but that was because we—" Elissa looked up wildly and bit her lip. Her face grew suddenly hot as Margaret pursed her lips and lifted an eyebrow. "Because he knows I'm in love with him," she amended quickly. "He feels guilty."

"Good. I raised him to have a conscience," she said curtly. "That's right, I was with his mama since he was just a boy. What morals he's got, I put there, no thanks to her. I took over where his dad left off. Poor old fellow, he couldn't take her everlasting roving eye. He was a good man."

Elissa studied her silently. "Is his father still alive?"

Margaret smiled gently. "Very much alive. He's in a nursing home in Phoenix—a good one. We correspond, and I tell him all the news about once a month."

"Oh, shouldn't you tell King?" she asked worriedly.

"Honey, Kingston would go crazy. He thinks his father deserted him, and he's never wanted anything to do with him. I wouldn't dare confess what I've been doing."

"But his father will die one day," Elissa argued.

"It's not my place to say anything," Margaret replied. She searched Elissa's pained eyes. "You could, though. He might listen to you."

Elissa laughed weakly. "I wonder." She stared at the emerald ring on her finger. It felt cold, an empty gesture to appease his guilt, to satisfy his sense of responsibility. Her eyes closed. Last night it had all seemed worth it. In the cold light of reality, with her mind back in control of her body, it seemed wrong. How could she have done it?

It had been a last desperate gamble, she thought miserably. To make him so enslaved that he'd get over Bess. But it hadn't worked. Bess was still number one in his thoughts. It seemed that she always would be.

"If you want him, fight for him," Margaret said gruffly. "You've got an advantage she doesn't. He likes you. All he really feels for her is pity and some leftover affection. She was like a child when she and Bobby got married. Kingston helped her over those first few quarrels."

Elissa studied her slender fingers. "Liking isn't enough."

"Neither is pity," Margaret said, and got up. "Now, you eat a good breakfast. We've got to build up your strength. If Bobby stays in the hospital for any length of time, we'll probably have ourselves a houseguest."

With a sinking feeling, Elissa watched Margaret's broad back disappear. She hadn't considered that King might bring Bess here. But on second thought, of course he would. And what a perfect opportunity for Bess to get through his defenses. And what in the world was Elissa going to do to prevent it?

Sure enough, a few hours later, King came in with a weeping, pale Bess in tow. Bess was still in jodphurs, gloriously sexy in the expensive silk blouse she wore opened to the deep cleavage between her breasts. Her honey-blond hair in a delicious tangle around her shoulders, and she was clinging to King as if he were a lifeline.

"I'll take her upstairs," King said, glancing at Elissa. "Call Margaret to help her undress, would you? Have you got a nightgown she can borrow?"

"Yes, of course," Elissa said dully, following them. "How's Bobby?"

"He'll be all right," he said, his arm protective around his sister-in-law. "His leg's broken, and he's got a hell of a headache, but he'll be out in a few days."

"Thank God," Elissa sighed. But nobody seconded that, least of all the two people in front of her.

She had only two nightgowns with her, but she spared the blue one for the opposition. Margaret gave it a sinister look as she carried it into the second guest bedroom to the tearful blonde.

Elissa slowly wandered back downstairs. Margaret was getting Bess some soup, and King, forgoing all the pressing business he'd been attending to without a thought to Elissa's lack of company, was proving he had all the time in the world for Bess. And why not? Elissa thought miserably. He loved Bess.

King ate his supper on a tray in Bess's room, to Margaret's blatant fury, leaving Elissa to eat alone or with the housekeeper.

"Idiot!" Margaret flared as she put a bowl of stew in front of Elissa. "Blind man!"

"Don't start feeling sorry for me," Elissa murmured. "I went into this with my eyes open. Nobody dragged me here. On the other hand," she added quietly, staring at the empty symbol on her ring finger, "I think I might see about a flight back to Miami. I'm only going to be in the way here."

"You can't go," Margaret huffed. "If you do, they'll be here alone, and I won't have that kind of gossip." She glared at Elissa. "Your parents wouldn't appreciate your doing that kind of thing, either. No, ma'am, you're stuck. I'm sorry, but there isn't a thing you can do and still live with your conscience."

Ah, Elissa thought, but you don't know what I'm already living with. You haven't a clue. But she didn't say it. Conventions or no conventions, she was getting out of there. If she didn't, seeing King and Bess together was going to kill her. She was brave but not suicidal. Her heart was already breaking.

King still hadn't come out of Bess's bedroom when Elissa went upstairs. Gritting her teeth, she looked in the door, which Margaret had apparently left open.

King was sitting beside the bed, holding hands with a radiant Bess, and they were talking about Bobby. Elissa felt sick all the way to her toes just looking, and then she heard what they were saying.

"I feel so guilty," Bess was saying. "But I couldn't help it, Kingston. You know how he treats me. I'm so alone. He's never going to change; we both know that."

"The horse was a stallion. I've warned him not to try to ride it," he told her.

"But it was because I told him I wanted a divorce," Bess burst out, and Elissa felt her blood run cold. "Oh, Kingston, I can't go on living with a man who doesn't love me anymore. It's so much worse now, and when I'm with you—"

Elissa knocked abruptly on the door; she couldn't bear to hear any more, and it would look as if she were eavesdropping if she waited any longer. They both jerked around, looking stunned by her unexpected appearance.

"How are you feeling?" she asked Bess, schooling her voice and face to show nothing but polite interest and friendliness.

Bess moved restlessly and pulled her hand from King's. "Oh, I—I'm feeling much better, thank you," she stammered. Her face colored. "I'd forgotten you were staying here."

"Under the circumstances, that's quite understandable," Elissa said gently, forcing a smile. "I'm sorry about Bobby, but I'm sure he'll be fine."

"They'll let him go home in a few days, they said." Bess sighed, then grimaced. "Back to his papers and business calls. He was already raving because they wouldn't let him have a telephone."

Elissa hesitated, unable to look at King. "Well, take care. I'll say good-night."

She went out, feeling her heart breaking inside, and stiffened when she heard King murmur something to Bess and follow her. She stood in front of her door, waiting for him, her back carefully straight.

"I'm glad she's going to be all right," she said, smiling, but she wouldn't meet his eyes. It was just as she'd predicted when she'd said back in Florida that she wouldn't marry him. She'd said that Bess might be free one day, and now it was going to happen. Elissa had represented an urge he couldn't control, but now she was an embarrassment, an obstacle. She stared down at the ring on her finger and knew how he felt and what he was thinking. If only he'd waited a few hours....

"She wasn't hurt," he said curtly. "Just upset. But I had to go to her."

Her, not his brother. She noticed the wording even if he didn't. "Of course."

He hesitated, which was unusual. "Elissa..."

She turned, forcing a smile. "Yes?"

"About last night..." he began slowly.

"Oh, yes. Last night." She pulled off the emerald ring and, taking one of his hands, pressed it into the palm. She stared at his closed fingers, feeling their strength and warmth and remembering all too well how they felt on her bare skin. She closed her eyes and wanted to die of the shame. "This is what you wanted, isn't it?"

He took a sharp breath. What did she mean, what he wanted? For God's sake, they'd made love. She'd told him she loved him. They were going to be married. So he'd brought Bess home—what else could he do? Surely, after what they'd shared the night before, Elissa didn't think he was still struggling with a hopeless passion for his sister-in-law?

"What I wanted?" he shot at her angrily. "Did I ask for the damned ring back?"

"Don't tell me the thought hasn't crossed your mind," she returned, staring at him accusingly. "I heard what Bess said, King," she confessed. "About divorcing Bobby. And maybe it's for the best. If they can't get along, and the two of you are... Well, I'm sure it will all work out," she added, lowering her eyes to his broad chest. The first few buttons were open, and involuntarily she wondered if Bess enjoyed touching him there as much as she did.

She turned away. She was about to burst into tears, and that would never do.

He stared at her as if she'd lost her senses. She'd agreed to marry him, and now she was backing out. Of course, he'd thought he wanted Bess, and now Bess was talking divorce. The obstacles to their union would be removed. And yes, he'd once thought he wanted that. But not now. Not anymore. He wanted Elissa, desperately, and here she was, throwing his ring back in his face. He felt suddenly, unreasonably angry.

"And what about you?" he demanded, hands on his hips.

Her chin lifted as she opened the door to her room. "What about me?" she asked curtly.

"You could be pregnant," he said bluntly. He sounded as if he wanted to throw things, starting with her.

"If I am, it's my problem, not yours."

"To hell with that!" he burst out. "It's my problem, as well, and don't you forget it."

His sense of responsibility, she thought miserably. "All right," she said quietly. "But there probably won't be a problem. I'd like to leave tomorrow."

He had to take deep breaths. His eyes flashed at her. "So that's it, is it? A quick one-night stand and you're off? You agreed to marry me, remember."

"That was before," she threw back. "I don't want to marry you anymore. I don't want to become like Bess, tied to a man who doesn't love her, who barely notices she exists! No, sir, not me. That isn't what I want to do with my life. What kind of marriage would it be if every time Bess calls, you go running?"

"Bobby was injured," he reminded her. "I had to go."

"To her," she agreed, lifting her head. "You didn't even ask if I wanted to come. Bess needed you, so you went."

"Of course I went," he ground out with failing patience. His dark eyes flashed at her. "Bess falls apart in a crisis. And if my little brother can't take care of her, I feel responsible for her," he added, recognizing without quite realizing it that he was articulating what had been his own feelings all along. "Anyway, damn it, you aren't making sense."

"On the contrary, I'm finally making perfect sense. I've finally opened my eyes," she snapped. "I can see what's ahead, and I want no part of it. Bess is frail and helpless and needs protecting, is that right? And I'm tough and insensitive and I don't need anybody?"

"That's how it seems to me, lady," he bit off, totally confused now and losing his temper. "You handle yourself just fine without help. You always have. You're too damned independent."

It wounded, but she smiled so that he wouldn't see. "It beats begging people to notice you," she said with a poisonous smile.

"When did you ever have to?" he demanded.

"The minute Bess got within thirty miles of you," she shot back. "And if you're bothered that I might die of love for you, you can forget that, too. I'm *un*infatuated! Why don't you go and let Bess cry on you some more? I've got packing to do."

Elissa's blind stubbornness was making him see red. "What will you tell your parents?" he asked coldly.

She took a deep breath. "That I got homesick. What else?" She closed the door behind her and, as an afterthought, locked it. When she heard him stomp off down the hall, she blushed at her own conceit. As if he'd try to come to her, with Bess so handy. She crawled onto her bed, still dressed, and cried until there were no tears left.

By morning, she'd salvaged a bit of her pride. She dressed in one of her own flamboyant creations, a stunning white pant suit with a red silk blouse. She wore heels, as well—red, to match the blouse—and carried a stylish white purse. Her long hair was pulled back into a bun, her makeup carefully applied. She looked sleek and sophisticated, a woman of the world. The fantasy was finally real, but now that she had it, she no longer wanted it. She wore rose-tinted sunglasses to camouflage the ravages of tears.

But she was a trouper. She'd learned from her parents that it always got darkest just before the dawn, so she glittered like sunlight as she joined Bess and King at the breakfast table.

"Well, good morning, glories," she bubbled, glancing from King's dark, shocked face to Bess's pale one. "Isn't it gorgeous traveling weather? Margaret, I'll just have toast and coffee, thanks. I don't manage airplanes very well on a full stomach."

Margaret sighed. "You're still going, then?" she asked, revealing that she knew what was going on.

"Of course," Elissa said brightly. "I made reservations a half hour ago. I've got two hours to get to the airport, and

I've ordered a taxi to take me there. Fortunately Jack's Corner is large enough to have one."

"I'll drive you to the airport," King said curtly.

"You will not," Elissa told him. She even smiled. "Don't be silly. You'll have to go to the hospital and see your brother."

"I'm getting a divorce," Bess said quickly to Elissa.

"Yes, I heard," Elissa said, as if it didn't bother her in the least. "It's probably the best thing for both of you, too. I'm sure you'll find someone much more attentive than your husband. He did seem rather too busy for you."

"He works very hard," Bess said defensively, and King glanced at her curiously.

Elissa only smiled. She thanked Margaret, who had deposited a cup of black coffee and two honey-brown pieces of buttered toast at her elbow.

"Do you have a headache?" King asked Elissa.

"Yes," she replied, touching the sunglasses. "But nothing bad enough to prevent me from leaving, if that's what's bothering you."

"For God's sake!" He hit the table with his fist, and Bess jumped. "I haven't asked you to leave!"

"Like hell you haven't!" Elissa gave as good as she got, glaring across the table at him. "I'm not blind! I'm nothing more than an embarrassment to you now. You can't wait to get rid of me!"

"I asked you to marry me!" he said shortly.

Bess's eyes widened, and her mouth flew open.

"Marry you? I'd sooner have—have Blake Donavan!"

"Then go get him, honey. He's available!"

She got up, shaking all over, wanting nothing more than to pick up a chair and hit him over the head with it. Black-eyed devil, sitting there as arrogant as an Indian chief, bursting with bad temper. Well, hers was just as bad, and he wasn't bulldozing over her ever again.

"Thanks, I might just do that," she said, her voice shaking. She turned and stormed back upstairs to finish packing. She'd left the coffee and toast untouched, unable to bear seeing King and Bess together again.

Margaret came up to get her when the taxi arrived. "I wish you wouldn't go," she grumbled.

"I can't fight her," Elissa said simply. "He cares about her in a way he'll never care about me. It isn't something he can help."

"But, honey, what about you?" Margaret asked gently, her eyes so caring that Elissa burst into tears and was gathered up like a child to be comforted. "There, there," Margaret cooed. "He'll come to his senses one day. Men get a little blind sometimes, and Bess has always been special to all of us. He's a little sidetracked right now, but once he's had time to miss you a little, he'll be along—you mark my words."

"Think so? I don't." Elissa wiped her eyes and nose on a handkerchief and crumpled it back into her purse before she readjusted her dark glasses. "There. Do I look terrible?"

"Not at all. Keep your chin up," Margaret advised. "Don't let them see you break down, even if you have to bite your tongue through. Poor Bobby, helpless in the hospital..."

"Poor Bobby may see the light if he can't get to his business for once," Elissa muttered. "What a pity he didn't look sooner; he might have saved himself some heartache."

"I suppose so. Well, you have a safe trip."

"I will. Thank you for being so good to me."

Margaret studied her quietly. "It's easy to be good to nice people. I hope we meet again someday."

"We probably won't," Elissa said, "but thank you for the wish."

She grabbed up her carryall and started downstairs. When she reached the hall, she heard voices in King's study. They stopped, quite suddenly, as she started past the open door, and a moan drew her attention. She glanced into the room and saw Bess in King's arms, smiling up at him.

It hurt, if possible even more than what had already happened, and she hurried past the room to the front door.

"Who was that?" King said, frowning as he heard the front door slam.

He moved away from Bess to open the curtain and look out, just in time to see Elissa dive into the waiting cab and slam the door before it roared off down the driveway.

"Oh, for God's sake," he grumbled. "I've got to go."

"Must you?" Bess asked, uncertainty in the soft eyes that looked up at him. "We were just going to talk."

"And we will. Later," he replied. He let out a slow breath, sensing that she'd already come to the same conclusion that he had; that his near involvement with Bess had been a sense of responsibility and tender affection on his part and desperate loneliness on hers. They'd work it out later, he was sure, without any hard words being spoken. He touched her blond hair lightly. "You're a lovely woman, Bess," he said gently, "but I've got a bad case on the woman who just walked out the door."

Bess sighed. "I guess I knew that already." She looked up at him. "It's just...well, I..." She faltered, trying to explain her own confused intentions.

"Don't fret," he said, smiling at her. "When I get back, we'll have that nice, long talk, and then we'll go see Bobby. Okay?"

She smiled wanly. "Okay."

He got into the Lincoln and proceeded to set new speed records driving to the airport. Damn. Elissa had probably seen him with Bess and drawn all the wrong conclusions. He was going to have to do some fast talking to smooth over this misunderstanding. He could only imagine how much her conscience was smarting over what they'd done together. Vividly remembering, he went hot all over.

Almost two hours later he caught up with Elissa while she was waiting to board her flight.

She looked up, her broken heart cracking all over again at the sight of him, ruggedly jean clad and visibly impatient. The image almost shocked her into smiling, but the pain was still too sharp. She didn't get up. She sat there, her dark glasses in place, and looked at him as if he were some insect.

He sat down beside her, glancing at the flight attendants who were just entering the walkway to the plane. "I have to talk to you," he said curtly.

"We've talked," she said calmly.

"What you saw wasn't what you think," he began.

"Your private life is none of my business," she said simply. "I'm not interested."

"Will you listen," he gritted. "We've only got a few seconds."

"Then you'd better make your speech short," she replied.

He drew in a steadying breath, gripping his temper tightly to keep it from exploding all over again. All in all, his patience was being sorely tried. He seized upon the first thing that came to mind. "If you won't marry me, fine. But if you find yourself pregnant, I want to know immediately," he told her. "Promise me this minute that you'll get in touch with me, or so help me, I'll phone your parents and tell them the whole sordid mess."

Sordid. So that's how he thought of it. Perhaps it was sordid. A little back-alley overnight affair that he'd forget soon enough when he and Bess were married. Her heart was breaking. She had only a little pride left, and it was in tatters. He knew that she loved him, and that hurt most of all.

"I'll get in touch if anything happens," she said finally, the words dragged from her. "And in case you're afraid I'll be eating my heart out over you, save your pity. Whatever I felt for you, it certainly wasn't love."

He stiffened and felt himself going cold. "That's a lie," he said, his voice quiet and deep.

"Love isn't part of sordid affairs," she said, her voice starting to break. "That's all it was, just a ... a cheap little roll in the hay!"

"No," he said softly, his eyes fierce. "Never that."

She turned away, clutching her bag. They were calling the first-class passengers aboard. She was next. She got to her feet. "I have to go."

He caught her arm, but she moved away and wouldn't look at him. "Elissa, damn it ..."

"I have to go," she repeated. "So long, cowboy."

"For God's sake, will you listen to me?" he demanded, oblivious to the curious stares they were getting as they faced each other.

"No." She laced the single word with mocking contempt, and her blue eyes dared him to make her change her mind.

He let go of his temper with a word that turned her ears red, and she walked away without looking back. He took off his hat and slammed it to the floor, damned it to hell, damned her with it and stomped back down the concourse. Let her go. What did he care? She didn't love him—she'd said so. It was just a "cheap little roll in the hay." His dark eyes got darker, and his pride felt lacerated at her careless reference to the most beautiful experience of his entire life.

Still cursing, he came home hatless and ran head-on into Margaret, who looked like an entire invading army about to launch an attack. "So you ran her off, did you?" Margaret glared at him. "Congratulations. The first woman who ever cared anything about you and not your money, and you get rid of her. I don't know what's come over you. And here's Bobby's wife, and—"

"Shut up!" King threw at her, his eyes dangerous.

"Jackass!" she tossed off. "You don't cow me! Maybe Bess is scared stiff of you, but I ain't!"

He glared back at her. "What do you mean, scared stiff of me?"

"She took off upstairs the minute she saw you walk in the door. And she never once opened her mouth at the breakfast table when you and Elissa got into it." She harrumphed. "That poor little thing's got no spirit at all. Not like Elissa. You'd have Bess crawling in a month's time, if she didn't cut and run first. Or don't you remember what a hell of a mean temper her father had when he drank? Of course, you can control yours, most of the time, but that child is carrying deep scars. A man like you is the last thing she needs!"

As if he hadn't realized that already, he thought furiously. Elissa was gone, and he felt sick, and here was Margaret, giving him hell. He glared at his housekeeper with black frustration.

"And where's your hat?" she demanded.

"At the airport," he retorted. "Catching mice."

"*Your* hat probably could," she muttered. "It would have to be pretty damned mean to sit on you!"

He sat down with a cup of black coffee, which he wished were whiskey. He felt empty and hollow and cold. Bess was still upstairs, and he thought about what Margaret had said. Perhaps Bess was afraid of his temper, he thought idly. But Elissa wasn't, he recalled with a faint smile. She was more than equal to his angry outbursts, most of the time. She was equal to him in other ways, too. He closed his eyes and saw her, felt her, as she was that night, her body lifting to his, her eyes wild and passionate, moaning as he held her to him, crying out his name in aching fulfillment.

He got up, his body on fire. Bess paused at the doorway, hesitating. He glanced at her. She was blond and beautiful, but when he looked at her, he saw only Elissa's laughing blue eyes and black hair.

"Well?" he asked curtly.

She hesitated. "Are you angry with me?" she asked.

The harshness left his face. She was a child, after all, in so many ways. He went to her, taking her gently by the shoulders, smiling.

"No, of course I'm not," he said gently. "I couldn't stop Elissa. She thinks I'm out of my mind over you and that you're leaving Bobby to marry me. I couldn't make her listen, and I'm frustrated, that's all."

"It's my fault, isn't it?" she asked, searching his eyes. "I'm sorry. I was so lonely. And you took me places and talked to me and even listened," she added with a wistful smile. "I guess I got drunk on attention. But I'm sorry if I've messed up your life."

"Don't worry. I'll sort it all out somehow," he said.

She stared at his shirtfront. "Elissa loves you, doesn't she?"

"I thought she did," he replied quietly. "Now I'm not sure."

She looked up again, smiling at him. "I liked her. She isn't the least bit afraid of you. She bites back."

He laughed. "Yes. She gives as good as she gets. That's one of the things I like best about her." He searched her face. "Do you really want a divorce?"

She sighed. "No," she said finally. "I love the stupid man to distraction. If only he'd wake up and realize that I never married him for money. I wanted *him*—I still do—and he's too busy making money to notice."

"Then why," he asked slowly, "don't you tell him?"

She blinked. "Tell him . . . that?"

"Of course."

She shifted restlessly. "Well . . ."

"Chicken," he taunted, his dark eyes sparkling.

She burst out laughing. "All right. Why not? Things can't get any worse, can they?"

He took her arm. "Where there's life, there's hope," he muttered. He was still wondering how to deal with Elissa's defection. She'd tried to reduce what they did together to something sordid and wrong, and he wished he'd gone about things in a more conventional way. He should have picked her up and carried her off to a minister. Now she was determined not to care about him anymore, was determined to put him out of her life. Did she still think he wanted Bess? How could she be so crazy?

He followed Bess out the door, frowning fiercely. He'd have to give her some time to cool off, to figure out that they couldn't live without each other, that they needed each other. And knowing Elissa, she'd have to come to those conclusions her own way in her own sweet time.

Eleven

Elissa didn't go home to her parents. She wasn't quite ready to face them just yet. Instead, she boarded the next flight to Jamaica. Since King was going to be busy with Bess now, it looked like the best time to tie up a few loose ends.

She went to his villa first and got Warchief, then left without a backward glance. She wasn't ever going to see the villa again. She'd made plans.

Warchief made eyes at her and flapped his wings while she packed. She couldn't accomplish everything in one day, so she took her time. There were forms to fill out to allow her to take Warchief back to the States, and there was the real-estate agent to see. She was going to put the cottage up for sale. After what had happened, she never wanted to come to Jamaica again.

It was like leaving home, because she'd grown to love it, but she'd have to find someplace else for a second home. Especially since pregnancy was a real possibility. She still hadn't decided what to tell her parents. She just couldn't bear telling them the truth.

She stayed in Jamaica for three days. Then, with the necessary forms filled out, she took Warchief to the airport in a sturdy pet carrier and left the island behind. Warchief was the one reminder of the past that she couldn't bear to give up.

Hours later, she pulled up in front of her parents' home. Her father was busy in his study, working on his sermon, which he always started on Fridays. Her mother was in the kitchen, and her head jerked up when she saw what Elissa was carrying.

"Oh, no!" Tina wailed. "It's the green mosquito!"

"Now, now," Elissa said gently. "He grows on you."

"That's what I'm afraid of," Tina muttered, nibbling her lip and frowning.

Elissa set his carrier on a chair. Warchief took one look at Tina and began to whoop and blaze his eyes and make cute little parrot noises.

"I love you!" he cried. "Cute, you're cute!" He gave a wolf whistle, and Tina, who'd never seen a parrot except in exotic pet shops, was charmed.

She dropped to her knees and peeked into the carrier. Warchief wolf-whistled again and blazed his eyes, and Tina laughed.

"You gorgeous bird," she enthused. "I'd love to hug you."

"I wouldn't," Elissa murmured dryly. "He gets excited when he's close to people. You could lose an ear, a nose—"

"I get the idea," Tina chuckled and rose. "What about his cage?"

"It's outside, in the car."

Tina looked out the window. "How did you squeeze it into that subcompact rental?" she asked.

"With great difficulty," came the reply. "But I did."

Tina cocked her head and stared at Elissa. "Wait a minute. He was in Jamaica, wasn't he?" she asked, nodding toward the parrot. "So how is it that he's with you, when you were in Oklahoma? And where's Kingston?"

"This is going to be an interesting story," Elissa said. "So do you mind if I get the things out of the car and change clothes? You can make coffee, and then we'll talk."

Tina sighed. "Uh-oh."

Elissa nodded. "That's one way of putting it."

"I'm sorry, darling."

"It's just as well I found out now," Elissa replied, looking and sounding worlds more mature than she had when she'd left. "I might have married him and ended up ruining his life."

"He asked you to marry him?" Tina asked.

Elissa nodded. "He gave me a ring," she said, smiling at the memory of the fragile thing. Then she burst into tears. "Oh, Mama, I had to give it back," she wailed, going into the taller woman's outstretched arms. "He's in love with his sister-in-law, and she's getting a divorce, and he only found out after he'd given me the ring. I had to let him go—don't you see? He'd have hated me for tying him down!"

Through all that muddled speech one thing was clear: that Elissa loved her man desperately and had given him up for love of him. Mrs. Dean smiled. "There, there, darling," she cooed, "you did the right thing. Loving isn't loving unless you have the strength to let go when you have to."

"I'm so miserable," she said brokenly. "I went to Jamaica and arranged to sell the cottage and got Warchief. Is it all right if I stay here for a while?"

"Honey, of course," Tina said, shocked. "Why wouldn't it be? This is your home."

Elissa lifted her tear-stained face to her mother's. She wanted to tell all, but she didn't know if she could bear to. Her eyes filled with new tears.

Tina Dean brushed the damp hair from her daughter's eyes. "I think this would be a very good time for you to have a talk with your father," she said with a smile. "Do you know the old saying that you never really know people until you're in trouble? Well, you're about to get an education in human frailty. Come on."

Elissa puzzled over that on the way to the study, where her father was sitting behind a desk, glaring at a legal pad and frowning.

"Look who's home," Tina said brightly, exchanging a pointed look with her husband.

"Hello, my darling." Her father beamed. "Home for a visit?"

"Maybe to stay awhile," she said. And then she burst into tears again.

"Uh-oh." Mr. Dean sighed and glanced at his wife. "Trouble in paradise, I guess?"

Tina nodded. "I thought it might help if you told her about that young minister and the unmarried couple. You know the one?"

He smiled, reminiscing. "Oh, I do indeed. Make some coffee, will you, dear?"

"I'll do that little thing." She went out and closed the door.

Mr. Dean came around the desk to hug his daughter and deposit her in an easy chair. He perched himself on the edge of his desk and studied her wan, tear-stained face. And then he smiled warmly.

"Elissa, I want to tell you about a young man I knew, oh, about twenty-five years ago," he began. "He was a cocky young brute, just twenty-three at the time. He was good with his fists and not very concerned with the world or even his own future. He came back from Vietnam half out of his mind on alcohol, and he robbed a grocery store and had the bad fortune to get caught."

He studied his neatly shined black shoes. "Well, to make a long story short, he went to jail. And while he was there, sure that God and mankind had given up on him, a young visiting minister took an interest in him. Now this young hoodlum," he added brightly, "had an eye for beauty, and he liked the ladies. And there was a lovely young girl with whom he was deeply in love. They'd gone, as the saying goes, a bit too far of an evening, and she'd gotten into a family way. So there she was, all alone, her lover in jail and a baby on the way."

He sighed. "The young minister found a capable lawyer to defend the young man. He got him off, since it was a first offense, then proceeded, in turn, to find the young man a job, get him married as quickly as was feasible to the young lady and move them into a small apartment."

Elissa smiled, her tears drying, sure that the young minister had been her father. "What a nice fellow," she murmured.

"Yes, I thought so, too," he sighed, returning the smile. "To finish, the young man was so grateful for what the minister had done that he entered a seminary and undertook to repay the man by carrying on his good work."

"And the minister, I daresay, was delighted with his handiwork."

Her father had a sad, faraway look in his eyes. "Well, not exactly. You see, the minister was in a reserve unit, and it was called up for duty in Vietnam. The young hoodlum I mentioned came out of combat without a scratch, but the minister stepped on a land mine the very first day he was in Da Nang." He sighed, a sound resonant with regret. "He was killed before that young man he'd rescued could get in touch and tell him that he'd decided to take the cloth."

Elissa felt a chill down her spine. "It was you," she whispered.

He nodded. "Me and your mother. I was twenty-three; she was twenty." He leaned over and took her hand, holding it tightly. "And now you know why we've sheltered you, don't you, my girl? How well we understand the passions of youth. All too well, I'm afraid." He smiled at her gently. "Now tell me all about it, and maybe I can help."

She burst into tears. In all her life, she'd never been so proud to be his daughter. "I didn't know," she whispered.

"Sometimes," he replied, "we have to fall into a hole to touch the sky. The important thing is to realize that we're never out of God's heart, no matter what we do. And very often it isn't until we hit bottom that we reach out for a helping hand."

She hugged him warmly and sighed, feeling at peace for the first time in days. "I could use a helping hand."

"Here's mine. Lean all you like."

After she told him what had happened, he took her into the kitchen, where they joined her mother for a cozy supper of cold cuts and iced tea. Not one word of censure was spoken.

Her mother seemed to know it all without a word from her husband. She smiled at Elissa with loving warmth. "Don't worry," she said gently. "There's nothing to be afraid of."

Elissa cupped her hands around her glass. "I could be pregnant," she said, putting her most delicate fear into words.

"Does he know?" Tina asked.

"Oh, yes," she said, looking up. "He made me promise to get in touch with him if that happened. But I can't see that it would help, to back him into a corner. He loves Bess. I can't tie him to me for all the wrong reasons."

"A wise decision," her father remarked. "But I think you underestimate the gentleman's feelings. Infatuation dies a natural death without anything to feed it; he'll get over Bess soon enough—if he's even still interested in her, that is."

"But he's got her now. She's going to divorce her husband," Elissa protested.

"Is she?" Mr. Dean looked at her over his glasses and grinned. "Well, we'll see, won't we? Eat your ham, darling."

She glanced from one to the other. "Aren't you upset?" she began hesitantly.

Tina lifted her thin eyebrows. "About what, dear?"

"The baby, if there is one!"

"I like babies," Tina said.

"So do I," her father seconded.

"But it will be..." Elissa hesitated.

"A baby," Tina finished for her. "Darling, in case it's escaped your notice, I've brought quite a number of unwed mothers into the congregation in years past, and the children have been raised in the church. Little babies aren't responsible for the circumstances of their birth. They're just babies, and we love them. Now do eat your ham, Elissa. For all we know you may already be eating for two."

Elissa sighed. She'd never understand them, but she certainly did love them. "What's your sermon going to be on?" she asked her father.

He looked at her gently. "On learning to forgive ourselves, after God has. Sometimes He punishes us much less than we punish ourselves, you know."

She flushed, wondering how he'd learned to read her mind so accurately. "I imagine we'll all learn from it, then," she murmured.

He winked at his wife. "Yes, I hope we will," he replied, and then he concentrated on his meal.

Warchief was back in his cage soon afterward, making enough noise to wake the dead. Elissa carried him into her room, saying a quick good-night before she closed the door.

"Be quiet, or you'll get us thrown out!" she raged at him.

"Hellllp!" he screamed. "Let me out!"

"Go to sleep," she muttered, pulling his beak toward her to kiss his green head. He made a parroty sound and wolf-whistled softly. She kissed him again, putting the cover over his cage.

As she slid into bed, minutes later, she wondered how King was and if he was happy now. She hoped he was. She hoped, too, that she wouldn't be pregnant. Despite the fact that she wanted his child very much, it wouldn't be fair to tear him between Bess and her own baby. For his own happiness, she had to let him go. She turned her face into the pillow, thanking God for loving parents and the hope of a new beginning.

But hope wasn't a good enough precaution. Six weeks later, after horrible bouts of morning sickness and fatigue, she went to her family doctor to have the necessary tests. And he confirmed her pregnancy.

She didn't tell her parents. Despite their support, which she knew she could count on, she had to come to grips with her situation alone. She went downtown to a quiet restaurant and drank coffee for two hours, until she remembered that coffee wasn't good for pregnant women. She switched to diet drinks and then worried about the additives in them. Tea and coffee and most carbonated drinks had caffeine, herbal tea nauseated her, and she hated plain water. Finally she decided that her choices had to be decaffeinated coffee, milk and Perrier. Those should carry her through the next several months.

The thought of the baby was new and delicate, and she sat pondering it through a fog of confusion. Would it be a boy or a girl? Would it have her coloring or King's? She smiled, thinking about dark eyes in a dark complexion and holding the tiny life in her arms and rocking it on soft summer nights.

The more she considered the future, the more appealing it became. She wouldn't have King, but she'd have a tiny part of him. Someone to hold and love and be loved by. Maybe that was her compensation for a broken heart. She smiled, overwhelmed by tenderness. She could still work;

pregnancy wouldn't hamper designing clothes. And her parents weren't going to throw her out in the street, although she worried about the impact her unwed-mother status was going to have on her father's congregation. She might get a cottage farther up or down the coast to prevent any gossip from harming his career. He'd find it hard to get another job at his age, despite his protests. He loved her, but she loved him, too, and she wasn't going to be the cause of any grief to her parents. Well, she'd think about that later.

Right now, the thing was to get back on her feet. She'd grieved so for King that she could hardly function. She had to learn to live with the fact that he wasn't coming after her. She'd spent the past few weeks gazing hopefully at the telephone and jumping every time it rang. Cars slowing down near the house threw her into a tizzy. She checked the mailbox every day with wide, hopeful eyes.

But there were no phone calls from Oklahoma. No visitors. And no letters. Eventually even her stubborn pride gave up. King finally had Bess, and Elissa was well and truly out of his life. So she began to make plans of her own. She was going to move someplace far away, and she wasn't going to tell anyone where she was going, not even her parents. She'd write to them, but she'd find one of those forwarding-address places that would confuse the postmarks. Yes, she had to do this on her own. She and the child would grow close over the years, and someday she'd tell him about his father.

That was when she remembered that King didn't know where his own father was and had always blamed the man for running out on him. She'd decided when Margaret told her about it that one day she'd tell King where his father was and make sure that he got to sit down and talk with him, to hear his side of it. But for now, she didn't have the right to deny King at least the knowledge of this child. She'd promised.

She went home, resigned to do the right thing, no matter how much it hurt. Bess would be there, surely, whether or not the divorce was final. Maybe they were preparing for the wedding already. She hesitated, but in the end she reached for the phone and called the number King had once given her in case she needed to reach him at the ranch.

Her parents were visiting a sick member of the congregation, so it was a good time to make the call. She didn't want them to see her go to pieces when she tried to tell King what had happened.

It rang once, twice, three times, four. She was about to hang up when a breathless, familiar voice came over the line.

"Hello?"

"Bess?" Elissa faltered.

"Oh, it's Elissa, isn't it?" came the enthusiastic reply. "Kingston isn't here right now, I'm afraid, but . . ."

Elissa paused. "Do you know where he is?"

"Not offhand, but I can take a message."

"No. Thank you." She hesitated, desperate to ask if the divorce had gone through. She settled for, "Is Bobby doing all right?"

"He's already back at work," Bess said, her voice oddly soft, "cast, crutches and all. I . . . are you sure I can't take a message for Kingston? I'm not sure he'll be home tonight, but I could—"

"No. I'm glad your . . . I'm glad Bobby is doing well. Goodbye."

"Wait!"

But she hung up, trembling all over. So now she knew. Bess was living with King.

She almost let it go at that and made her plans without trying again. But that was the coward's way out. She phoned his office, only to be told that he wasn't in and they didn't know when to expect him. She left word, but the secretary didn't sound reliable. As soon as she hung up, she wrote a terse note and dropped it in the mail, addressed to his Oklahoma City office. Perhaps he could find time to read it, she thought unreasonably, and went back to her designs.

She'd finished her collection, mailed the completed designs to Angel Mahoney and picked out a nice town near St. Augustine to move to. She packed her things, careful not to let her parents see the baggage. She'd leave in the morning. It had been over a week since she'd mailed that note to King, and she was sure he'd seen it by now. Perhaps he didn't want any complications and was going to ignore it. That wasn't like him, but men in love weren't always rational, she guessed. He'd wanted Bess for a long time, and now he had her. It wasn't his fault that he wanted to look ahead and not behind him.

Warchief was quiet these days, almost as if he knew he'd lose his home if he kept being noisy. He purred at Elissa and talked to her, but he'd stopped making such wild noises at dawn and dusk. She wondered if he was sick.

Heaven knew, she was. The morning sickness hadn't let up, and she was beginning to feel pregnant. Her slacks were tight, and her breasts were sensitive. She grinned at all the little disadvantages. None of them mattered, because she was going to have a baby and love it so much that it would feel as wanted as she always had.

She settled down to bed that night, leaving her parents sitting up to talk. There was a full moon and a scattering of stars, and she closed her eyes with a sigh. King would be seeing that moon out his window in Oklahoma, probably with Bess lying beside him. She hoped Bess would be kind to him. Tears stung her eyes. Instead of getting easier, bearing the knowledge that she'd never see King again was getting harder every day. But she'd better get used to it, she chided herself. Forever was a long time.

About two o'clock in the morning, she and Warchief were awakened by a thunderous knocking on the front door. With a white chenille bathrobe thrown hastily over her nightgown, she rubbed her sleepy eyes and stumbled to the door, calling, "Who's there?"

"Kingston Roper," came the gruff reply.

She fumbled the door open. With his jacket slung carelessly over his arm, his tie hanging haphazardly around his neck, and his face hard and drawn and in need of a shave, he looked haggard and weary but devastatingly handsome. And Elissa wouldn't have cared if he'd been covered in mud.

"Come in," she said, fighting down the impulse to throw herself at him, trying to appear calm when her heart was beating her to death and her breath was stuck somewhere below her collarbone.

He stood looking at her as she shut the door again, his eyes dark and troubled and oddly hungry. He didn't move, as if riveted to the spot, staring.

"What was that noise? Oh, hello, Mr. Roper," Tina said, smiling at him from the door of their room off the living room. "You look exhausted. Elissa, there's some decaffeinated coffee you can reheat, and some of that cake I made. You can put Mr. Roper in the spare room if he's staying. Good night, dear."

She closed the door again, and King turned back to Elissa.

"I'll heat the coffee if you'd like a cup," she said quietly.

He searched her face, looking for any sign of welcome, but there was none. His eyes dulled. He'd hoped so desperately that she might have missed him even a fraction as much as he'd missed her. He'd stayed away deliberately, denying himself the sight and sound and feel of her all this time to try to make her miss him, to make her see the light. And he knew that it hadn't worked. He looked at her and thought he'd die of emptiness if she sent him away. He followed her into the kitchen without another word, as cold inside as an empty tomb.

Twelve

King sat down in the chair Elissa indicated and watched her move around the kitchen, slicing cake and heating cups of coffee in the small microwave oven. She looked delicious. Glowing. Wait a minute—didn't they say that pregnant women glowed? He took a slow breath, feeling warm all over with the possibility of it, with possession in his eyes as they followed her. He'd win her back somehow. He had to.

"I didn't expect you," she said.

"I went back to the office tonight to check some figures," he said as she placed mugs of steaming coffee on the table, along with saucers and forks and slices of cake. "I've been in Jamaica," he added, glancing up.

"Have you?" She nibbled at her cake.

"Your cottage had a young redhead in it," he remarked. "She said her parents had bought the cottage from you. Warchief was gone, too."

"I have him here," she said. She took another bite of the cake, still without looking at him. "You found my letter tonight, I guess?"

"Buried in a stack of bids," he confirmed. He left half his cake uneaten and leaned back in the chair with his coffee cup in his hand, studying her. "Was that note the best you could do?" he added. "A terse 'Need to talk to you when you have time. Best wishes, Elissa'?"

She flushed. "I'd already tried your ranch and your office. Nobody seemed to know where you were."

"Nobody did, for a while," he said. He didn't mention that the past few weeks had been pure hell. His temper had become so vile that it had already cost him two of his best junior executives. So much for testing that absence-makes-the-heart-grow-fonder business, he thought angrily. She didn't look any the worse for wear, but he sure as hell did. He stared at her coolly. "Are you having any morning sickness?"

She almost dropped the coffee cup.

"Well, why else would you bother to contact me?" he chanced. "It wasn't out of love. You told me how you felt when you left," he said curtly, his dark eyes glittering at her across the table. "The only possible reason was that I'd made you pregnant. So here I am." He didn't mention that he'd practically bought an airline to get here that fast.

"There was no rush," she said. "I've got everything worked out. My parents know," she added softly. "They didn't make accusations or rage at me or even try to shame me. They said…" She bit back tears. "They said people are human."

"Oh, God," he whispered roughly. Though he himself was delighted—surely she'd reconsider and marry him now—he hadn't thought about how her parents would take the news. He wasn't surprised that they'd stand by her, though. They were good people, and they loved her.

"It's all right. I make more than enough money to take care of myself and the baby. And you can visit if you like," she told him. "But I'd rather you waited awhile," she said, lifting tired eyes to his. "I don't want people gossiping, and it's the last kind of complication you need right now."

He stared at her blankly. Bess said Elissa had called, so didn't she know that Bobby and Bess were back together? "It's my baby," he said simply. "I want to take care of you both."

"I don't need taking care of, thank you," she said with forced calm, remembering that he hadn't bothered to make a move toward her in seven weeks and that Bess was now living with him.

He exhaled angrily, leaning forward to pin her with his dark, quiet eyes. "I'm responsible for you," he said. "This is all my fault."

"I'm not blaming you," she replied. "That isn't why I contacted you. I gave my word that I would, if it happened."

He stopped breathing for an instant. "That's the only reason you got in touch with me?"

Her eyebrows arched with practiced carelessness. "What other reason would I have had?"

He wanted to throw something. "You loved me once," he growled.

"Oh, I've gotten over that," she assured him, rising to put the empty cups into the sink and praying that he wouldn't see through the fiction of what she was saying to the agony underneath. She swallowed down tears. "It was just infatuation. I was pretty naive, you know, and you were very experienced. Any girl can lose her head with a sexy man. I just happened to be a little too naive. You see—" She turned to tell him a few more choice lies, but he wasn't there. Seconds later, she heard the front door open softly and close. Then a car engine roared once, and she heard the vehicle drive away.

It had no sooner pulled away than the phone rang. What a night, she thought miserably. At least, thank God, she'd kept her composure. King hadn't guessed how she'd grieved for him, and that was something. He'd leave her alone now, and she and the baby would be each other's world. King wouldn't have to sacrifice his happiness with Bess on Elissa's account.

She lifted the receiver on the second ring, hoping her parents hadn't been disturbed again. "Hello?" she said, wiping away a tear.

"Elissa?"

It was Bess. Elissa glared at the telephone. "If you're looking for King, you're too late. He's on his way back to you—I made sure of that—and you don't have to worry. I won't bother him again. The baby and I will manage just fine."

"Baby?" Bess sounded shocked.

"King will tell you all about it, I'm sure. It's no concern of his anymore."

"Please don't hang up," Bess said suddenly.

"I can imagine what you have to say to me, but—" Elissa began quietly.

"No, you can't," Bess interrupted softly. "I'm sorry. I'm so sorry. I've loused things up for you and Kingston, and I almost destroyed my own marriage, all because I couldn't tell Bobby the truth, couldn't tell him what I really wanted. Elissa, Bobby and I aren't getting a divorce. I finally got up enough nerve to swallow my pride and say what I felt, and now we're staying together. I was sure Kingston would have told you by now. He was the one who convinced me to talk to Bobby," she added, stunning Elissa into silence. "I tried to tell you when you phoned that time, but you hung up. Bobby and I were visiting him."

Elissa could hardly breathe. "Visiting?" she echoed hoarsely.

"I guess you had a pretty good idea what was going on all along, but most of it was just in my mind. Poor Kingston was truly caught in the middle, all because he felt sorry for me. Well, he's big brother again, and I do adore him. But if you'd seen him these past weeks, you'd know that he didn't give a hang about me—not the way you thought. He's nearly worked himself to death, taken crazy chances with the livestock and that new sports car of his—he's gone hog-wild, Margaret says. Margaret tried to get him to go see you, but he wouldn't. He said he couldn't go until you asked him to, because that would mean you still loved him. Margaret says he loved you all along, only he didn't know it. I think he knows it now. I just hope I haven't done anything to take his last chance away from him. I think he'll go crazy without you, and that's the truth."

Elissa was still trying to find her voice. "I sent him away," she whispered tearfully. "I thought you and he were getting married. I couldn't let him sacrifice his own happiness...just because I was pregnant."

"Oh, Lord, I hate myself!" Bess groaned. "Listen, can't you go after him?"

"I don't know where he's gone," Elissa wept.

"Well, if he comes here, I'll send him back," Bess promised. "Now you go get some sleep. Don't worry too much; it isn't healthy for the baby. My gosh, Bobby and I will be uncle and aunt. That sounds so nice. Get some sleep, honey. Everything will be okay—I promise."

Elissa's heart warmed at the compassion in that soft voice. "I'll be all right," she said. "You'll let me know if he shows up there?"

"Of course I will. And good luck."

"Thanks." Elissa hung up with a sigh. Lately, all her luck seemed to be bad. She went to the sink and bathed her flushed face. It didn't help a whole lot, so she went out the back door and onto the quiet beach. Maybe a walk would help clear her mind.

She wandered along in her robe, hardly seeing where she was going for the pain. What irony, she thought miserably. She'd sent him away, and for what?

She didn't notice the silent figure near the dune until he spoke. "You'll catch cold," he said, his voice deep and lazy.

Elissa whirled, catching her breath, to find King sitting there, smoking a cigarette. He was in his shirt sleeves, his chest bare where the white shirt was unbuttoned, his dark hair untidy.

"What are you sitting there for?" she asked shakily. "I thought you'd gone."

"Oh, I started to," he agreed pleasantly. "And then I realized I had no place to go."

"There are hotels in Miami," she faltered, wrapping her arms around herself as she drank in the sight of him, her eyes adoring every hard, powerful line of his body in the darkness.

"You don't understand." He put out the cigarette. "You're the only home I have, Elissa," he said quietly. "I don't have any other place to go."

Tears stung her eyes. She'd never dreamed, even when Bess was telling her those things, that he cared that much. Trembling a little with mingled excitement and fear, she went to him and dropped to her knees in front of him.

"I thought it was Bess," she said simply.

He looked up at her, his eyes dark with possession. "So did I, at first," he returned. "Until you started taking me over, that is. First my body, then my heart. In the end, all I felt for Bess was compassion and responsibility. I could have told you that when you left, but you wouldn't listen," he said gruffly. "Seven weeks I've stayed away, hoping against hope that you'd miss me. I broke speed records getting here tonight, and for what? To be told you didn't give a damn!"

She stopped the tirade with her mouth. Poor wounded man, she thought. She slid her arms around his neck and felt him tremble as she pushed, gently unbalancing him. He fell against the dune, and she fell with him, her softness melting over him, her eyes red from crying, her mouth tasting of salty tears.

"Will you listen?" he ground out against her lips. Then he groaned and captured her, enfolding her against the warm strength of his body. His mouth opened under hers. She felt the deep penetration of his tongue, the throb of his heart. He was hers.

She nibbled his lower lip, lifting her head to stare down at him, her eyes adoring, sure of him. Her hands smoothed back his hair, and she smiled as she touched him with confident possession.

"Are you, by any chance, trying to seduce me?" he whispered. His heart was pounding, and his body was making insistent statements about what it wanted. He tried to shift her so that she wouldn't feel how vulnerable he was, but he couldn't budge her.

"Just lie still," she chided. "I know you want me, so there's no use trying to hide it."

He glared up at her. "Rub it in," he muttered.

She bent and kissed his eyelids with aching tenderness. "Were you going to sleep on the beach?" she whispered.

"If that was as close to you as I could get, yes," he said angrily.

He was a hard man, she thought lovingly, lifting her head to look at him. A real handful. But she could manage him. They'd been friends a lot longer than they'd been lovers, and now she knew how to throw him off balance, as well.

She sat up, opening her robe. "I want to show you something," she said without the least bit of self-consciousness, although she peeked down the beach, knowing her parents were eventually going to come looking for her. Under the robe, she was as she slept, bare except for a tiny pair of blue briefs.

He stared at her, stunned, as if he couldn't believe what he was seeing.

"This is what you did to me," she whispered tenderly. She took his hands and held them to her minutely swollen waistline, watching the incredible expression that tautened his face as he touched her.

"My child..." His voice was soft, deep, reverent.

She gathered his head against her sensitive breasts, tears stinging her eyes as she rocked him, cradled him, feeling his lips touch her, though not in a sexual way. His hands smoothed over her under the robe as he brought her against his body, holding her so close that she could barely breathe. And she cried, because he cared and because she loved him.

"You little imp," he whispered, nuzzling her warm throat. "I'm so crazy about you. I would have carried you home to Oklahoma in my arms, walking."

Her lips touched his face, her breath catching as he turned and put his mouth with aching tenderness to her breasts.

His hands came up to touch them, to cup them. He moved, laying her down gently on the robe so that he could look, could explore the new contours of her body with his child tucked under her heart.

"Our baby," he whispered, his fingers trembling as he lay beside her in the darkness with the surf crashing behind them.

She trembled with the profundity of the moment. "I know exactly when we made him," she whispered.

He met her eyes. "So do I, to the very second. I meant to, even though I was temporarily confused about Bess. Do you know that the minute I got home from putting you on that plane, I patched up her marriage? She admitted that she loved Bobby, that she was just lonely. She'd never stopped loving him, but she was afraid to tell him how she really felt. She did, though, and now they're closer than ever. They're even talking about having babies."

She laughed. "She called me a few minutes ago. She wanted to clear the air."

"Nice woman. I'm glad she and Bobby have finally gotten their act together." He looked down into her eyes, searching. "Do you know how I feel, or do you want the words?" he asked gently.

"Have you ever said them before?" she countered.

He smiled ruefully. "No. But I never wanted to before, either."

"When did you know?" she asked.

"I knew how *you* felt when you were willing to give yourself to me in Jamaica." He laughed at her startled expression. "That's right, tidbit, I knew before you did. But there was Bess, and I didn't think I wanted that kind of involvement. But when I saw you lying in bed in that sexy nightgown, and I got hot and bothered like I never had before..." He bent and brushed his mouth over hers, reveling in its soft, trembling response. "After that, bad went to worse. I didn't really want to seduce you at the ranch, but my body got the best of me."

"Yes, so did mine," she sighed, nuzzling his cheek. She closed her eyes. "It's been hard living with it, King," she whispered.

"How do you feel about starting over again?" He touched her abdomen. "And decide quick, would you? I think he's already growing."

She grinned at him, drunk with happiness. "As if I could have stopped loving you." She laughed. "Seven weeks, damn you!" She hit him.

He crushed his mouth down on hers, suddenly all man, all domination, burning her with his ardor. "Damn you, too," he growled, his lips hard against her mouth. "Calling it a 'cheap little roll in the hay,' when I'd never loved a woman that way in my life. Sticking a knife in my pride, my heart. I went off like a wounded animal to lick my wounds, then went to Jamaica with my heart in my hands to offer to you...and you'd gone. You'd sold the cottage and taken Warchief, and the real-estate agent said you hated the cot-

tage and everything connected with it." His eyes narrowed.
"I guessed that meant me, too. So I went back to Oklahoma and drank myself into a stupor, then set about working myself to death."

"While I was sure you were going to marry Bess," she murmured. "I knew how you felt...."

"How you thought I felt," he corrected. He kissed her softly. "I slept with you for one night, and it ruined me for any other woman. You've haunted my dreams ever since. An innocent, and you gave me the first total fulfillment I've ever had."

She smiled against his mouth, bristling with pride. "Sitting up, too," she murmured, and she blushed wildly.

"Don't smile about it, you brazen hussy," he taunted. "I needed my head examined. I prayed every night that you'd end up pregnant," he confessed, "because I knew you'd send for me. Your sense of honor would force you to. And then I'd come to you and take care of you and find some way to make you love me again." He traced her breasts, watching them tauten in the moonlight.

"Don't forget," she whispered, loving the sensation, "that my parents are just down the beach."

He kissed her softly. "I hadn't forgotten," he said with a rueful smile. "I'm not about to give them any more cause to resent me."

He helped her back into her robe and pulled her onto his knees, cradling her.

"How could they resent the father of their very own grandchild?" she whispered, her mouth brushing warmly over his. "He's going to be just like his daddy." She smiled. "Tall and dark and handsome and gentle."

"Blue-eyed," he whispered, tilting her warm mouth up to his.

"Brown-eyed," she whispered back, and drew his lips over hers.

A long time later, he lifted his head. "Elissa?"

"What?" she murmured dreamily.

"I think we have company."

She looked up. Her father was sitting on one side of them, his knees drawn up under his bathrobe, watching the surf. Her mother was on the other side, similarly clad, humming.

"Lovely night," Mr. Dean remarked.

"Lovely," his wife agreed.

King and Elissa burst out laughing. "The marriage license and the rings are in my jacket pocket," King told them. "All we need is a quick blood test and a quiet little ceremony, which we hope you'll perform. You, uh, might have noticed that we've rather jumped the gun," he added with a sheepish smile.

"She likes kosher pickles in her corn flakes, and he wonders if we've noticed that they've rather jumped the gun," Mr. Dean addressed his wife.

"Yes, dear, I heard." Mrs. Dean grinned.

"And in case it crossed your mind," King murmured, glancing wickedly down at Elissa, "we've been controlling those interesting impulses that led us to this delicious complication. We've just been trying to decide what color his eyes will be."

"I like girls," Mr. Dean suggested.

"What's wrong with a boy?" Tina asked innocently.

"Maybe it will be both," Mr. Dean remarked. "Her appetite has been extraordinary."

"I'd like twins," King murmured, his eyes shining with everything he felt as he looked at the slender, beautiful woman in his arms. He glanced up at her parents, who were on their feet now. "I'm sure you'd rather things had worked out a little more conventionally, but I guess I had to learn how to love."

"You seem to have the hang of it now, son," Mr. Dean said dryly.

"It's not all his fault," Elissa muttered. "I sort of forced him into it."

"You did not," King flashed.

"I thought you told her the facts of life," Mr. Dean murmured to his wife.

"I thought you did," came the dry reply.

"Well, we might try again. Come on, children, we'll have coffee and discuss some details," Mr. Dean said, sliding an arm around his wife's waist. "Nice boy."

"I think so, too." Mrs. Dean stopped, glancing behind as King gently helped Elissa to her feet. "There's just one thing, Kingston," she murmured, frowning. "I shouldn't really ask, but can you support her, working in a garage? If you need any help, we'll do what we can."

King burst out laughing. He drew Elissa close to his side and fell into step beside her parents. "While we have that coffee," he told them dryly, "we'll have a little talk about the oil business."

Two weeks later, King and Elissa were back in Jamaica at his villa, Warchief happily installed in his cage while his owners set out for a new and delicious experience on the beach. It had been a learning period for them both, getting to know each other without the barriers of uncertainty and mistrust.

Just before they'd left for Jamaica again, Elissa had even found a way to tell King about his father, still alive and in a nursing home. King had listened to her, then sat staring into space for a long time. Minutes later, he'd gone off to use the phone. When he came back, he'd looked thoughtful and pleased. She'd later learned that he'd spoken to the old man and had promised to go and have a long visit with him after the honeymoon. It was a milestone, Elissa had thought.

And speaking of milestones... She hesitated as they walked out onto the damp sand.

"Someone will see us," she squealed as King stripped he out of her robe and nightgown, leaving her bare and beau tiful on the white beach.

"The only person who might lives in the cottage, and she's away for a week. I checked," he said, chuckling and pausing to strip out of his own robe. "Come on. You'll lov this."

He led her into the warm, rippling water, and she felt i swallow her up like a satin embrace. She gasped at the ex quisite freedom of it while she swam and floated and fi nally wound up close against a smiling King.

"Now I see why you like it," she whispered. "It's.. incredible."

"Yes, isn't it?" But he wasn't looking at the water. Hi hands were busy under its surface, doing things to her body that made her gasp and cling to him and cry out.

He took her cry into his mouth, taking full advantage o its position to explore it in a silence that quickly grew ho and hungry. He lifted her into his arms and carried her ou onto the beach, putting her down gently in the center of a huge beach towel. He stood over her, his body fully aroused his eyes, dark and wild, devouring her as she lay there. " want you," he whispered hoarsely.

"Then why don't you come down here and do something about it?" she whispered huskily, stretching in a way tha made her tremble.

He eased down completely over her, his hands gently tangling with hers, letting her have most of his weight, feel ing the bare saltiness of his skin over every inch of hers.

"You look like you did the first time," she said softly.

"I was hungry then, too," he murmured, finding her mouth. "Starving for you, by then. I still am. But it's...hard to describe." He lifted his head, shifting his hips to make her gasp. "Patience," he teased softly. "I want to talk first."

"Talk fast," she pleaded.

He nipped her lower lip and teased it with his tongue. His hands were on her waist now, her hips, moving her body against the hair-roughened contours of his in a kind of love play he'd never used with her before. She caught her breath, clutching at the broad shoulders above her, the fires kindling deep in her body.

He looked down the length of them, smiling at the tremors claiming her long, slender legs, shudders that he could feel along with her changed breathing. "There are hundreds of paths to fulfillment," he whispered, moving his eyes slowly back up to catch hers. "This is a new one." He bent, putting his mouth to her breasts.

"I thought . . . you wanted . . . to talk," she gasped when he took a hard nipple into his mouth.

He laughed huskily. "I'm not sure I can just now. Oh, baby," he breathed, positioning her, hungrily assaulting her mouth, dragging his body against her until she was on the verge of tears with the sensations he was arousing.

Her nails scored him, and she moaned. "I'm sorry," she whispered shakily. "I didn't mean to . . ."

"Bite, claw, scream," he ground out against her mouth. "Whatever you need, whatever you want, I'll give you. Tell me."

She did, astonishing herself with her own shameless whispers. She looked up at him then, seeing his eyes blazing with love, his face taut with passion but tenderness, as well. She threw back her head and nearly wailed as the first wave hit her and she went into spasms of hot, almost unbearable pleasure.

Somewhere in its midst, she felt him move, felt him still, heard him cry out above her and then shared the delicious echo of her own shudders.

It was a long time before she could breathe again. The stars came back into focus over his shoulder, and she felt the warm wind off the ocean on her damp, bare skin.

"The first man and woman—it must have been like this for them," she whispered in his ear. "Alone in the world, under the sky, joining."

"Joining," he whispered. "Cherishing. Becoming one." He lifted his damp head and searched her rapt eyes. He kissed her softly, touching her belly. "Is he all right?" he whispered. "I didn't mean to get so rough."

"He's fine," she whispered back, smiling.

"It excites me," he said quietly, "having my child inside you, knowing I helped create him." He breathed deeply. "What I wanted to say to you," he murmured, resting half his weight on his forearms without moving away from her, "is that when we make love, it isn't just sex."

She smiled. "Yes, I know." She adored him with her eyes, the excitement growing again. "It's an expression of love, isn't it, King? It always was, even the first time."

"Reading my mind again," he murmured contentedly. "I've noticed that even your parents seem to do that."

"I think they're pretty super," she said.

"So do I. That being the case, it might not be a bad idea if we adopted them." He toyed with her lower lip. "What with his lizards and her crime busting, they need looking after."

"Mother almost wept with relief when she found out we were bringing Warchief back with us, did you notice?" She grinned. "She thinks he's a giant green mosquito."

He grinned, too. "He bites, all right. But he's learning to sing lullabies—have you noticed?" he added on a frown.

"I'm teaching him," she confessed. "I expect to have more than one child, you know. He can sing babies to sleep while I rock them."

His powerful frame trembled a little. "I like babies."

She shifted her hips very slowly, her lips parting, her eyes come-hitherish, feeling him begin to tauten. "So do I," she whispered. "And this time," she added, pushing at his shoulders until she got him onto his back and moved over him, "I'm going to show *you* something new."

"Elissa..." He held her hips, hesitating.

"Just relax," she whispered, looking like an imp, her eyes sparkling. "I won't hurt you."

She moved, and he groaned harshly. And then it was too late to protest. He felt his body being flung up against the sky, hearing her soft laughter, dying in the throes of a feverish struggle for control that even as he fought, he lost.

When his eyes opened, her face was there, smiling at him, loving him. He sighed. "Well, I guess there had to be a first time," he teased, exhausted. "And we are married, and it's a new world."

"Prude," she whispered, putting her mouth softly on his. "You're just afraid you'll get pregnant in this position."

He burst out laughing, holding her to him. "You enchant me," he whispered. "Tease me, torment me, burn me up. I love you so damned much, I can hardly breathe for it."

That was the first time he'd actually said it. Tears burned her eyes, and she buried her face against his chest, hugging him to her. "I love you, too," she whispered. Her eyes closed. "I always will."

His arms closed around her, and he sighed. "Have you ever noticed how close heaven seems when you look up at the stars?"

She smiled against the rough hair over warm, pulsating muscles. "I know how close it feels," she murmured, nuzzling his chest.

"Yes," he said gently, pressing his hand to her stomach as he folded her against his side. "So do I." He kissed her forehead with aching tenderness. "So do I, my darling."

Above them, a silvery drift of clouds passed over the waning moon. And back in the villa, a gravelly parrot voice was crooning the opening bars of "Brahms' Lullaby."

Silhouette Desire

COMING NEXT MONTH

#355 LOVE SONG FOR A RAVEN—Elizabeth Lowell
The choppy waters surrounding the beautiful Queen Charlotte islands had brought Raven and Janna together. But would their fiery love weather the storm?

#356 POSSIBLES—Lass Small
If Sara Moore was looking for husband material, Steven Blake had real possibilities. Despite her aloofness, Steve was determined to show her just how probable he could be.

#357 WHERE THE WANDERING ENDS—Sara Chance
Nicholas's life was based on stability, but Andrea was a free spirit. Still, he had captured her heart and urged her to settle down. Could their love survive clipped wings?

#358 NO HOLDING BACK—Candice Adams
Entrepreneur Patrick Cummins was interested in more than Elana Bradley's company, and as business took a backseat to romance, she wondered if she'd signed away her heart.

#359 FALSE PRETENSES—Joyce Thies
One look at Tricia Courteau, and G-man Paul Lansing knew he'd met his match. If she was a Mafia hit woman, then he was Paul Bunyan— but she was pretty enough to make a big man fall.

#360 RETURN TO YESTERDAY—Annette Broadrick
Felicia had only returned to Texas and Dane Rineholt because she needed his help. Searching for her missing brother would be dangerous, but did traveling with Dane pose an even greater threat?

AVAILABLE THIS MONTH:

Take 4 Silhouette Intimate Moments novels
FREE

Then preview 4 brand new Silhouette Intimate Moments® novels —delivered to your door every month—for 15 days as soon as they are published. When you decide to keep them, you pay just $2.25 each ($2.50 each, in Canada), *with no shipping, handling, or other charges of any kind!*

Silhouette Intimate Moments novels are not for everyone. They were created to give you a more detailed, more exciting reading experience, filled with romantic fantasy, intense sensuality, and stirring passion.

The first 4 Silhouette Intimate Moments novels are absolutely FREE and without obligation, yours to keep. You can cancel at any time.

You'll also receive a FREE subscription to the Silhouette Books Newsletter as long as you remain a member. Each issue is filled with news on upcoming titles, interviews with your favorite authors, even their favorite recipes.

To get your 4 FREE books, fill out and mail the coupon today!

Silhouette Intimate Moments®

Silhouette Books, 120 Brighton Rd., P.O. Box 5084, Clifton, NJ 07015-5084

Silhouette Desire

Available May 1987

Still Waters

by
Leslie Davis Guccione

If Drew Branigan's six feet of Irish charm won you over in *Bittersweet Harvest*, Silhouette Desire #311, there's more where he came from—meet his hoodlum-turned-cop younger brother, Ryan.

In *Still Waters*, Ryan Branigan gets a second chance to win his childhood sweetheart, Sky, and this time it's for keeps.

Then look for *Something in Common*, coming in September, 1987, and watch the oldest Branigan find the lady of his dreams.

After raising his five younger brothers, confirmed bachelor Kevin Branigan had finally found some peace. He certainly didn't expect vibrant Erin O'Connor to turn his world upside down!

D353-IR

For the millions who can't read
Give the Gift of Literacy

One out of five adults in North America
cannot read or write well enough
to fill out a job application
or understand the directions on a bottle of medicine.

**You can change all this by joining the fight
against illiteracy.**

For more information write to:
Contact, Box 81826, Lincoln, Neb. 68501
In the United States, call toll free: 800-228-3225

**The only degree you need
is a degree of caring**